NIGHTMARES OF MURDER

NIGHTMARES OF MURDER

by
Dana Pride

Everlasting Publishing
Vancouver, Washington
USA

Nightmares of Murder
by
Dana Pride

Library of Congress Control Number
2009900606

ISBN: 978-0-9778083-9-7

First Edition
Everlasting Publishing
P.O. Box 965
Vancouver, WA 98666-0965

Although this book is fictional, it was inspired by real events, real dreams, and real people. Thank you, Rose, for being one of those real people.

*Dedicated to my husband, who
always encourages me to write,
and to my dad, who reminds me
to pay attention to my dreams,
even when weeds are growing
up around his car and my mouth
keeps being full of gum.*

NIGHTMARES OF MURDER

SUNDAY

CHAPTER 1

Kori rushed around the corner in the dark night as quickly as she could, walking, though, not running, so she wouldn't arouse suspicion. She glanced at her surroundings without exposing her face. Nobody had seen her: no one knew what she had done. She had to get away from the scene immediately, away from the incident, away from the memory she had just created by being there. She had never before been in this area, in this part of town. This was not the type of place to come in the middle of the night – why had she come here? She hurried down the cold, shadowy street, past the tall brick buildings, her face looking at the ground. Steam rose from a nearby manhole as she scurried by it. Not another soul was on the street; but she couldn't risk running into a police officer who might ask where she was going or a good Samaritan who might try to offer her some help, or anybody at all.

Her life would never be the same. She had done the unthinkable. She didn't want to think about it. She couldn't stop thinking about it. Her mind and her conscience would never again be clear. From this night until the moment of her death, she would know she was guilty of murder. She had killed someone.

She couldn't remember the details of the murder. Who was this person? Why had she been there? How had she killed this person? She didn't know; she just knew she had ended a person's life, and she had had no right to do that. She would have to carry this burden with her for the rest of her life, a burden so heavy it made her struggle just to put one foot in front of the other. She began to concentrate on her feet, left in front, pulling right to the front, pulling left to the front, wondering how all her life she had been able to walk without consciously making each foot take turns pulling her entire body forward. Her feet were so very heavy, as if each one were pulling a ball and chain.

She had murdered someone. She had committed the worst crime, the worst sin. Nobody else knew what a terrible thing she had done, but she knew it. She could never tell anybody. Now she would never be able to get married, because she couldn't marry a man and then keep such a horrible secret from him – and if she ever told him, he wouldn't be able to accept her. No, she could never tell anybody anyway. She turned another corner and inhaled the scent of fresh bread baking as she shuffled by a bakery. It smelled so good, much better than anything she deserved to smell. She should only be allowed to smell the odor of the garbage from the overflowing bin across the street or the rotting banana peel in the gutter. Oddly, she couldn't smell these things, she could only smell the bread, still, even though now she was more than two blocks away from the bakery.

She had to put as much room as possible between herself and the scene of the crime. Why couldn't she remember it now? What did the crime scene look like? All she could recall was rushing down several flights of stairs to get away from the dead body, escaping through a back door into an alley, and rushing between buildings to get to the street. She was so scared. She didn't want to be here. She didn't remember why she had come here or what had driven her to commit this crime. She was freezing on the outside but burning on the inside; so very cold, yet at the same time, she was on fire. She couldn't feel her lips or her fingertips. Her skin was growing clammy in the muggy darkness. She was so thankful she didn't meet anyone on the street – her hair was probably a frizzy mess by now. Wait, her hair should be the least of her concerns. If someone were to see her, she could be arrested! She quickened her pace.

As she scampered down the block, it seemed to lengthen. She instinctively knew she was heading in the direction toward her home, but how could she ever get there if she couldn't get to the end of this block? Was she going the right way? She had to get out of this part of town, to a familiar area she recognized, and at the same time she had to avoid being recognized. She suddenly had the feeling someone was behind her, getting closer to her. No, it couldn't be the person she had killed... but it could be someone who wanted to kill her! She had to get out of here!

MONDAY
CHAPTER 2

Kori awakened with a start. She sat up straight in her bed. It was just a dream! It had been just a dream. She hadn't murdered anyone; she hadn't just taken a man's life. She was alive, and he – whoever he was – was also alive. A huge sense of relief washed over her, although the realistic sights and smells and the chill of the night air from her dream still clung to her like a dampness after a walk on a misty day. No wonder she had felt lost and in an unfamiliar place – she had never been there. She had been dreaming.

She looked at the clock: only 6:42 a.m. She didn't go to work until noon; however, she couldn't go back to sleep now. This would be a good time to start her spring cleaning by moving her furniture and vacuuming the living room of her apartment. Well, maybe she should just move the furniture now and then vacuum a little later, after others in the building had awakened. She could sweep and mop the kitchen floor and do the dusting.

She began to get out of bed, but she was so tired! Her legs ached from hurrying across town, down all those streets and alleys. She was physically exhausted after all the activity in her dream! She knew it didn't make any sense, but she also knew it was true. Her body was so tired, she couldn't get out of bed. She rolled onto her side and began to pet her cat, Tundra, who seemed to be very upset by the intrusion into her good night's sleep: Tundra, soft, smooth, real, live Tundra.

What was Kori going to do all morning? She was physically too tired to get out of bed, but she was too scared to go back to sleep. The nightmare seemed to be lingering just beneath her eyelids, waiting for her to return to those cold, dark, scary streets and that awful state of fear: fear not only because of what she had done, but fear that someone would discover what she had done.

What was the matter with her, anyway? She had no reason to fear, no reason to be afraid of going to sleep... and this would be the perfect time for her to start reading her new Nicholas Sparks novel. She entered his world for the next few hours, until it was time for her to get ready for work and come back to her own world.

CHAPTER 3

"Hey, are you somebody famous?"

Kori turned to see a tall, young man with curly, blond hair standing on his balcony, which overlooked the sidewalk leading to her apartment building.

"No," she called over her shoulder, as she trotted down the sidewalk to the parking lot.

"Yes, you are!" he yelled. "I've seen you before, on TV!"

Kori shook her head.

"You're somebody famous! I know you are!" he called.

Kori didn't respond as she unlocked her car door. She was probably the only person in town who locked her car, but she wasn't a native Dakotan. She had grown up in an area where doors were always locked.

"I know who you are! You ARE somebody famous!"

Kori smiled as she got into her car. She was too shy to become famous. She liked to be in the background, taking care of business, not in the spotlight. She drove to the TV station where she worked, which was only a few blocks from her apartment. She was considering, perhaps when the weather got warmer, she would walk to work for her first shift, then walk home and have dinner, then drive back to the station for her second shift.

She entered through the back door of the TV station and went to the control room where she worked. She loved her job. She was one of the few people in town who was paid to watch television. For the first portion of her first shift, when the network programs ran, she sat in the control room monitoring the signal, which came from New York, and she ran the tapes that played the local commercials and station breaks every half hour. Monday through Friday, she was paid to watch the soap operas every afternoon. Then at 3:30, she changed roles, from master control switcher to associate director of the news. At that time, she began to type all the news titles and graphics into the computerized character generator. During the 5:00 newscast, she accessed the titles and graphics as the director called for them, and he placed them on the screen at the proper time. At 5:30, her break began, and she ate dinner, went shopping or took a walk until 8:30, when she came back to begin preparing the graphics for the late news. She really loved her job. She was always around the famous people in town, although she wasn't famous. She was well informed of the local, national and international news, and she was respected for the job she did. She took her work seriously and she did it well.

"Hey Brad," she said to the young man sitting at the master control console. His shaggy blond hair flew out then settled around his head as he quickly glanced at Kori, then turned back to the master control switcher board. Brad had worked as the morning switcher at the station for nearly six years, and now he was being trained to work as one of the engineers.

"Hey, Kori," he said, "I got this break, then it's all yours." He pushed the remote button to start the tape machine in the tape room, then he pulled the mixer bar for a smooth transition from the program to the commercial.

"Nice switch," Kori said, as Brad recorded the time of the break onto the master log.

"It's been a quiet morning," Brad said. "The tape machine hasn't acted up and I haven't fallen asleep, not once. Hey, do you watch the workout program at 6:30? I started working out with them, and I feel great! What a great way to start the day!"

"You start working at 5:30," she reminded him.

"I know, but I zone out that first hour, for the farm report and stuff. Hey, did you hear about the new PA/AD job opening up? You gonna go for it?"

"Yeah, I heard about it, but I love doing the news."

"I heard the pay will be the same as yours, but it's a nine-to-five thirty, five days a week, and much less pressure."

"I'd have to actually work instead of watching the soaps," Kori said, as Brad played the station ID and then switched back to the network signal.

"When we go digital, you won't have to even watch the soaps. Everything will be in the computer," Brad said, as he stood so Kori could sit at the control console.

"Two things wrong with that statement," Kori said. "First, someone will still have to monitor the output, in case something happens with the computer, or the signal, or the weather, or if we have a power failure."

"Yeah, so true, too true," Brad agreed.

"And the other thing, do you think Mr. Buck will ever spring to go digital? Do you know how much it costs? More than he would ever want to spend. We'll be the last station on earth to go digital."

"You're right, they'll still need us."

"Well, even if they don't need you as switcher, they'll need you in engineering. I heard Ernie's going to retire pretty soon."

"Yeah, he's teaching me everything he knows. We'll need to get a new apprentice. Hey, maybe you should train for engineering."

"Me? No, I don't think so. I want to be available for any computer programming position, just in case they go digital."

"Good luck waiting forever for that! There's lots more pay in engineering. Plus, you could learn how to fix computers."

"Do I want to learn how to fix computers?"

The side door to the control room opened and Maureen, the news director and news anchor, stuck her head in through the doorway.

"Hey, Kori," Maureen said, "Did Jessie get back together with Marishka?"

"No, he's still in Europe, and Marishka still has amnesia," Kori answered. The members of the news team often popped into the control room for an update on the soaps, and they knew Kori never missed a minute of the programs. As a matter of fact, she hadn't missed a day of work in more than nine years. She had been at the station longer than most of her coworkers, except for some of the people in the front office, who worked in advertising and billing, but she didn't really know them. She worked with the production crew, the engineers and the news team; and she knew the soap opera stars as if they were her own family.

"What about Doc Lewis? Did he find out Kandy's baby is really his?"

"No, she changed her mind about telling him at the last minute, when she heard he got engaged to Carolyn and then Carolyn's brother decided he isn't gay so he might want to marry her."

"Okay, wow! Thanks for the update. So, we have a special story we're opening with tonight, and I'll get the graphics to you early since you'll probably have a lot of last minute sports scores."

"Thanks, I appreciate that," Kori said, as Maureen made her way back to the newsroom.

Brad went to the engineering room to work with Ernie, and Kori checked the schedule and the tapes to be sure her next commercial break was loaded in the tape machine, then she sat down to focus on the story of the hour. She watched four soap operas every week day: three one-hour programs, then a 30-minute program. When the local programming started at 3:30, another switcher, usually Barry, took over the master control board so she could concentrate on news preparation.

Kori looked at the wall of TV monitors in front of her, each labeled so it could easily be identified: the signal coming from New York via microwave transmission, which was the normal network signal they carried when they were carrying the network programming; the satellite feed from New York, which carried the same program but the signal wasn't quite as clear and was half a second behind the microwave signal; the East Coast feed, which was two hours ahead of their programming schedule; the outgoing signal, which showed the programming that was leaving the station; the off-air signal, which showed what viewers at home were watching; one monitor for each studio camera; one color monitor for the output from the production room; a color monitor for the character generator; one monitor for each of the seven tape machines and one for each of the two movie projectors. She turned up the volume of the off-air signal so she could listen to the same audio viewers who were watching at home could hear.

The program dissolved to a scene where a young woman stood with a bloody knife in her hand. Her face had an expression of horror that made Kori very uncomfortable. A chill ran through her entire body as Kori watched the woman begin to tremble.

"What have I done?" she asked aloud, looking at a point off the screen. "Is he dead? Did I kill him?"

Kori was mentally transported back to her nightmare. She knew exactly what the woman was feeling – shock, horror and the sinking feeling that she would never be the same because she had taken another person's life. She had ended a life. That person would never exist again – never speak, never move, never laugh, never love again. The images of her dream became real before her eyes, the streets, the buildings, the steam, the guilt, the chill: yet she couldn't remember killing anyone.

"Kori, ready for the break?" Brad asked, bringing her back to the control room. She glanced at the clock. Nearly twenty minutes had passed, and the network was going into its mid-program break, signaling the time when she would soon have to do her job: roll the tapes and switch from the network signal to the local tapes, run the station identification, and then rejoin the network signal as they returned to the program.

"Yeah, sure, everything is loaded," she said, glancing through the window into the tape room to be sure the tapes were still loaded in the machine. She sprang to action when she saw that the red light was not on, indicating that the machine was not in remote-ready mode. She flew out of her chair and through the door to the tape room, extended her arm and finger to press the button to set up the remote, then she leaped back toward the master control room, banging against the door as it swung back to smack her, she bolted through the doorway to push the start button and slide the fader bar just in time for the commercial to start, before the network went to black.

Brad stood calmly watching.

"Wow, that was an award-winning performance," he remarked. "If I didn't know how much of a thrill-seeker you were, I would have thought you weren't prepared for your break. Where were you, anyway? You looked like you were a million miles away. I know you weren't wrapped up in the story."

"I – I – um – I don't know, I guess I was just dreaming," Kori replied.

"Are you sweating?"

"No, I just..." She was sweating. "I just spaced out for a minute, I guess."

"Are you okay?" he asked, truly concerned.

"Yeah, I just didn't get enough sleep last night."

"Well, this is not the time to sleep. Everyone's going to be here at 1:00 when they start the interviews for the new job."

"Everyone? Be here? In here?"

"Well, I'm sure they'll bring the applicants through here for a tour, so you should probably be awake when they do."

"Thanks, I'll stay awake."

Brad left Kori alone in the control room and she recorded the times of the commercials on the log. She was upset with herself for her mistake – she prided herself on being fastidious and precise. She was not a person who made mistakes. That was one reason she was so good at her job – she paid attention to details and she was always alert. She wasn't a perfectionist – she just always did everything just right.

"And this is the master control room," she heard her boss, the production director, Jeff, say, as he opened the door. She turned to see him and his boss, Dared, the production manager, giving several people a tour of the station; most likely, the candidates for the new position. "This is Kori, our Associate Director of the evening newscasts, and right now, she is running the station," Jeff said. He had a baby face and alert eyes. Dared looked just like Art Garfunkel, with his fuzzy hair standing up on his head.

"Hi," Kori said with a shy smile. The three candidates smiled nervously but didn't say anything as the group moved out of the control room. The last guy to leave the room, a guy who looked like a short, stocky Jim Carrey when he was in 'Dumb and Dumber,' grinned and leered at her as he left. Kori shuddered. She was the only female in the production department, and all the applicants today were male. She hoped that guy wouldn't be the one selected for the position.

The afternoon passed quickly and soon the newscast was about to start. The station filled with news reporters, production crew members and directors. Kori typed the graphics into the character generator as quickly as she received them, including the last-minute sports scores and weather updates. Kori put on her headsets so she could hear Jeff, who was in the production control room, which was on the other side of the tape room. As he directed the news, he sat beside Tom, who ran the audio.

"One minute! Stand by on camera one," Jeff said over the headsets. "Stand by to roll tape. WHERE'S MAUREEN? She's live in less than a minute!"

"Here she comes," Don said. He was the floor director this evening. At this small TV station, eight people worked on the production team during the two nightly newscasts: Jeff, the director, who also switched the newscast, Kori, the associate director, who operated the graphics computer, Don, Sandy and Big Jeff, who worked in the studio as camera operators and floor director, Tom, who did the audio, Dennis, who ran the teleprompter, and Barry, who ran the tapes and switched the commercials. The news team had seven regulars who worked on the evening news. Both the news team and the production crew had a group of part-time people who worked on the weekend newscasts.

Kori glanced at the preview monitor to be sure she had the opening graphics in place while she reviewed her list of upcoming graphics. She had everything set in the usual order, but she was always ready for a last-second change of plans. The director could change the order – or call for a new graphic – at any time, so she had to be ready and alert. Normally during the newscast, only the director spoke through the headsets while the rest of the production crew kept their microphones muted, unless Jeff asked for a response.

Maureen waddled into the studio – she was nearly nine months pregnant – with a fast-food bag, her stack of news copy, and a huge smile on her face. She sat beside her co-anchor, Ken, whom, Kori thought, was appropriately named because he looked just like a Ken doll - and his head was about as empty as a Ken doll's head. He sat admiring his reflection in a mirror off-camera. He was so good looking: nice house, but nobody home. Kori really liked Maureen but she wondered what Maureen could possibly see in Buddy, her big, goofy husband, who was the sports director. Maureen stashed her food under the news desk and was organizing her paperwork as Jeff gave the final countdown. Maureen always had all her news stories, including extra fillers, if needed, on paper, just in case there was a problem with the teleprompter or the timing of any of the segments.

"Ten seconds," Jeff announced, both through the headsets and over the studio intercom. Kori glanced at the studio monitor and saw both camera operators straighten and tighten their shots on the co-anchors. Jeff always opened the newscast with a long shot from the unmanned third camera in the studio with the opening sequence of graphics, right after the pre-show teaser.

"Stand by camera one with a squeeze shot and teaser super." That was Kori's cue to have her first graphic ready to be used on the opening shot. All through the newscast she would have the upcoming graphic ready to be used live and the next graphic 'on deck' on the preview screen, ready to be sent to the live area when Jeff asked for it. He was the one who actually put the graphics on

11

the screen, while Kori made sure they were ready, spelled correctly, in the live area where Jeff could insert them.

"Stand by, camera one, mic on, take one, and cue her," Jeff said as he cut to Maureen.

"Good evening, I'm Maureen Zimmah. Our top stories tonight..."

"Teaser super in," Jeff said, indicating he was using the first graphic Kori had ready. For the rest of the newscast, Kori would be paying attention to Jeff's instructions. She could not let herself get distracted by what the newscasters were saying.

"Teaser out," Jeff said. "Give me the opening, stand by to roll tape. Three, two, one, roll tape. Stand by to take tape... take tape, opening graphic in, graphic out, stand by with a two-shot on two, camera two, tighten up a smidge! That's better, ready on two, take two, stand by on one... take one, give me Maureen's name, Maureen is in. Stand by with graphics for the lead story, name out, ready to roll the mayor story, camera two, tighten up on Ken, give me 'today,' roll tape, take tape, 'today' is in, it's out, here today, gone tomorrow... stand by for sound bite, sound up, cut her mic... give me Mayor Jordan's name, name in, name out, what happened to his hair? Looks like he stuck his finger in a socket. Is that a style for men his age? Give me Ken's name. Okay, stand by on two, camera two! Wake up! Straighten up and don't cut off Ken's head! You know he always sits tall when he starts reading! Better, much better, okay, turn on his mic, take camera two, cue him, cut sound on tape, Kenneth is in, Ken is out, give me a tight shot on one, not too tight, give her some room to breathe! Stand by on one, turn on her mic, one is on, stand by on two, take two, give me 'up next.' One, zoom out to a two-shot, stand by one, super in, super out, give me the weather teaser, take one, cut the mics, super in, roll tape, super out, take the commercial."

At this point, Barry switched the commercials while the rest of the crew prepared for the second segment. Barry organized the news tapes he would be rolling for the next segment while Kori prepared the graphics for the upcoming news stories. She paged through them quickly on the preview screen to be sure she had everything in order and spelled correctly, then she waited for Jeff to tell her which graphics he wanted to use first.

"Rob wants to do a weather warning off the top," Don whispered in the headsets.

"Maureen is okay with that?" Jeff asked.

Maureen nodded her head as Rob entered the studio and stood by the weather map.

"Do you have any specials from Rob, Kori?" Jeff asked.

Kori pushed the button to turn on her headset microphone. "No," she replied, then released the button to again mute her mic.

"Okay, just give me his name," Jeff said. "Let's get him on one." Jeff switched on the studio sound so Maureen could hear him. "Hey, Mo, will we keep the same order after Rob?"

"No, let's cut the dog story and Ken will follow Rob with the Bismarck piece," Maureen said, with a mouth full of French fries. She finished chewing and daintily wiped the corners of her mouth with a napkin.

"Okay, we'll come out on camera one on Rob, camera two, ready on Ken. Kori, give me Rob's name, let's see what he says, then let's be ready with the Bismarck supers. The dogs are out. Who let them out? Stand by on one."

"Ten seconds," Barry said.

"Stand by," Jeff said, "Rob's mic on, two, one, camera one is on, cue Rob… give me his name, Roberto is in, Roberto is out. Did he say possible ice storm? Oh, up north, in the great white north, that's okay… stand by with Kenny on two, camera two, you're going to cut his head off, that's better, Rob's wrapping up, Bismarck tape ready, Ken's mic on, take two, cue Ken, cut Rob's mic, stand by to roll tape, that's not the dog tape, right?"

"Bismarck," Barry said.

"Good, roll it, take tape, give me the Bismarck super, it's in, it's out, sound up on tape, keep Ken's mic on, he's coming back with a voice over, whoa! Who shot that? Mama, mia! Three old ladies at home just threw up."

Kori knew without seeing the tape that the pan had been way too fast. Jeff always used that phrase when the camera operators moved the camera too quickly. Their brand new field cameras only brought back as good a picture as the camera operators recorded. The video was clearly more defined than with the old cameras, but the new cameras didn't guarantee well-shot video. The news

13

photographers needed to have some talent and a slow and steady hand.

"One, give me Maureen. Stand by to come back on two, center him up, he shifted a little, two is on, cue him, Kori, get ready with the Moorhead supers, stand by on one, one, loosen up a little, she's bursting out of the shot, turn on her mic, ready on one, take one, stand by to roll tape, roll it, take tape, cut the mics, give me the first super, super in, super is out, next, it's in, it's out, how long is this tape? The time is crossed out on my sheet."

"Forty-two seconds," Barry said.

"Oh, we've got all the time in the world," Jeff said. "Give me the next super, it's in, it's out, stand by on two, get ready to give me the pizza supers, two is ready, five seconds, center him up, two! He shifted again! Stand by, two, Ken's mic on, two is on, cue him."

Kori shuffled her copy of the news notes to prepare for the next portion of the news and the weather and sports, her busiest time of the newscast. She needed to have each of the graphics ready in rapid succession during both the weather and sports segments, and often Buddy changed the order of the sports stories at the last minute. Buddy burst into the control room now, his face beet red. He was sweating heavily and he didn't even have on his jacket yet.

"You gotta get these scores in," he insisted, shoving a stack of papers at Kori.

"All of these?" Kori asked.

"Yeah, it's the playoffs, I'm leading with this. I need them all, in this order, then we'll go to the other stories in the same order as I gave you."

"Okay," Kori said, as Buddy flew out of the room.

"When we go digital, you won't have to type in his scores, he can just send them to you," Barry said, as a way of encouraging Kori.

"IF we go digital," Kori said, knowing she wouldn't have time to type in these scores until the commercial break started. "How long is the break?"

"This one's two minutes, the next one is only one," Barry told her, "but the first one has two promos, they'll probably cut them."

"Plenty of time," Kori said.

"Stand by to go to break," Jeff said. "Ready, roll tape, and we're out. Kori, I need the New York graphics."

"I've got the first one up, but Buddy just gave me a stack of scores he needs," Kori said into her headset, typing frantically.

"Oh, yeah, the playoffs," Jeff said. "Barry, how much time do we have?"

"It's a two-minute break, the last two are promos," Barry said, moving around the control room, shifting tapes and loading tape machines.

"Let's keep the first promo, cut the second one," Jeff instructed. Kori was glad to hear that – it gave her 90 seconds to type in the scores. She typed and saved, typed and saved, typed and saved the scores, glancing at the monitor occasionally to be sure she had no misspellings.

"This is it," Barry said, indicating that the final promo was airing before the end of the break. Kori continued typing frantically.

"Stand by on the floor," Jeff said. "Camera one, couple of changes, we'll come out on you, Mo's going to read two stories, then we're going to weather. Kori, keep typing until Rob comes up. We're dropping New York. I don't need Mo's name. Give me Rob's name, camera two, set up on weather. Barry, is the weather tape cued?"

"Yes, sir," Barry replied.

"Excellent, thank you, five seconds, stand by on one with her mic, mic on, three, two, one, take one, cue her, stand by on two."

Kori finished typing the sports scores just in time to call up the weather graphics. She liked doing the weather, because Rob was so organized and normally he kept everything in order, and also, she had little clouds and suns and snowflakes graphics, not just words and lines for supers.

"Give me Rob's name, it's in, it's out, highs and lows, they're in, they're out, tonight's forecast, it's in, get ready with tomorrow's, what? It might drop below freezing tonight? Don't wash your Cadillacs this evening, guys. Tonight is out, tomorrow is in, stand by extended, tomorrow is out, extended is in, stand by regional, extended is out, regional is in, trivia of the day, ready, regional is out, trivia is in, man! Can you believe it was twenty below on this day seven years ago?"

"Yeah, that was the day my vacation started, and our plane couldn't take off because the runway was iced over," Big Jeff said.

"Oh, yeah, I remember, the Twins' game was cancelled," Jeff said. "Trivia is out, stand by on one with Maureen. As soon as I cut to her, I need a two-shot on two. Turn on her mic, stand by to cue her when he's finished. Wrap him up, he's going over, wrap, wrap... and one is on, cue her, cut Rob's mic. Camera two! I need a two-shot, fast! Buddy has a lot to say, we've got to get into the break! Okay, I'll take that. Stand by on two, turn on his mic, take two, look at the love birds! She's smiling at him, but what's underneath? Do we sense a little tension here? Buddy is oblivious, as usual. Mr. Sports Fan can't tell his wife is foaming at the mouth. Stand by to roll tape, give me the sports teaser, roll tape, wrap him up! Take tape, we're out, cut the mics. Barry, how much time do we have?"

"One minute."

"Kori, do you have all the playoff scores in?" Jeff asked.

"Yes, I do."

"Excellent! Good job, gang, let's make it another perfect day!"

Kori called up Buddy's name super and then she prepared the sports scores to be shown in the order Buddy had instructed.

"Stand by on two with a tight shot of Buddy and his name – I'm going in with his name so we can get it out of the way and get to all the playoff scores – five seconds, tighten up a little, two, and one, get ready with a two shot for when we come back; no, make it a three shot, we're going to be out of time, have to drop the last national piece unless Buddy Boy cuts his segment short, mic on, take two, and cue him, his name is in, and it's out, what's with the green suit? He looks like a giant leprechaun, stretching his suit to the limit! Where's the rainbow? Looks like he just ate the pot of gold. Stand by with the scores – are they on a roll?"

"Yes, a roll," Kori answered.

"Okay, stand by to roll scores, and roll them, they're on, keep rollin,' rollin,' rollin,' who knows how to keep them doggies rollin'? We're on a roll, folks. Stand by to come back to Buddy Boy on two, dissolve to camera two and cue him. Give me the local coach interview supers, stand by to roll tape, okay, roll tape, sound up, take tape, Blastermeier is in, Blastermeier is out, last night is in, last night is out, how long is this bite? Seventeen seconds, how would you like the name Blastermeier? Wow, how many times did he just say 'basically'? Basically, I counted at least four from Basically

16

Blastermeier. Stand by with Buddy Boy on two, two is on, cue him, give me the high school supers, stand by to roll tape, roll tape, super is in, super out, next, it's in, it's out, next, it's in, it's out.

"Camera two, loosen up on Buddy Boy, you've got him boxed in, that's better, super is in, it's out, coming back on two, two is on, okay, give me the scores, he's going to read the national scores, Kori, follow him, super is in, just keep up with him, good, just keep up with him, here he goes, okay, last score, super scores are out, stand by to roll the tennis tape, roll tape, take tape, camera two, give me a two shot, two, tighten up a little on the love birds, no supers on this tape, give me the closing credits, stand by on two, as soon as the tape ends, whoa! This must be bad hair day! Look at that! Can you believe it? Is that mousse or is that a mouse on his head? Okay, here we go, mics up, two is on, cue them. Stand by to roll tape, teaser is on, take tape, and we're out. Cut mics. They're not coming back, we're out of time, give me the short credits, take credits, stand by to join network, you've got it, Barry. Thank you, crew, for another excellent show!"

The newscast was produced and directed without any technical errors for the seventh day in a row – they were counting. They didn't count the talent errors; they let the news department decide whether or not they were making mistakes or intentionally stammering, stuttering and mispronouncing words. The production crew's job was to make the live program technically perfect; they had no opportunity for a second take. Some members of the news team could get quite angry when technical mistakes were made, so the production team worked together to do their best to be error-free, and they were really on a roll now. Kori was exhilarated. Doing the show really gave her a rush. Everyone was in a great mood when they had a perfect newscast. As soon as the news ended, Kori was free for three hours, until it was time to prepare for the late night news cast.

Kori left the station and drove to her apartment so she could eat dinner and then return for her next shift. She thought about Maureen and Buddy, the news anchor and sportscaster who were married, going out to eat every night between their shifts, and her boss, Jeff, and his wife, Pat, who worked in the advertising department, going home to have dinner together. Kori wondered if sometime, somewhere, she would be sharing dinner with someone.

"You ARE famous! I KNOW you are famous! I've seen you before!" her neighbor called from his balcony as she approached the apartment building. He was not that someone, she already knew that. He was a lot younger than she was, he was tall and gangly, and obnoxious, not her type at all.

"No, really, I'm not," she said, shaking her head.

"Well, where do you work?" he asked.

"At the TV station."

"I knew it! I knew it! I've seen you on TV before! Haven't you been in a commercial before?"

"Well, I have been in a couple of commercials, but I'm not famous," she explained.

"Yes, you are famous! If you are in commercials, you HAVE been on TV! If you are on TV, then you are famous! What's your name?"

"I'm Kori."

"Kori, it's nice to meet you. Wow, I know a famous person! Hey, I'm Theo." He extended his arm over the balcony railing as if to shake her hand, but even his long arms couldn't reach that far. "Shake!" he shouted.

"Nice meeting you, Theo. See you later," she said, as she let herself into the building, before he could say anything else.

Kori had lived in the building for more than three years, but she didn't know any of her neighbors. The people were friendly, but she just didn't have anything to say to them. She went to work, and she kept to herself when she came home. She enjoyed cooking her dinner during her break, and by the time she got home after 11:00 p.m., her neighbors were probably asleep. On the weekends, she worked overtime whenever she had the opportunity. She even volunteered to work on holidays. She was never sick - she had not missed one day in all the years she had been at the station.

As she opened the door to her apartment, she realized that she was already quite sleepy. No, she couldn't even think about taking a nap now – she would surely oversleep and miss her shift. She could make something really good for dinner – like spinach pizza with homemade dough. She quickly assembled the dough ingredients and started the bread machine, setting it for 90 minutes while she fixed the sauce and chopped the spinach, onions, and feta cheese. She sorted through the mail while waiting for the bread machine to finish the dough process, avoiding sitting or resting, knowing that if she relaxed at all, she would slow to a stop. It was best for her to keep busy. What if she were to fall asleep and then she had that dream again? She decided to take a short walk to refresh herself. It had just been a dream, only a dream.

CHAPTER 4

"Hey, are you going to work at the TV station now?" Theo asked as Kori was on her way to the parking lot. Why was he always standing on his balcony? Didn't he have anything else to do? He was beginning to irritate her.

"Yes," she replied, hurrying down the steps.

"Hey, wait!" Theo yelled.

"I have to go to work," Kori called, as she passed a man who was going up the steps to the building.

"Hey, are you Julie Moore's brother?" Theo yelled at the man. "Because you look just like her. You look JUST LIKE Julie Moore. Man! Are you Julie Moore's brother?"

"No, I—"

"You're not? You're NOT Julie Moore's brother! Wow! You look EXACTLY like Julie Moore! How can you not be her brother? Are you sure you're not Julie Moore's brother? You look JUST LIKE Julie Moore, EXACTLY like her! You could be twins! Are you her twin brother?"

"Hey, man, I don't even have a brother," the guy said.

"You sure LOOK like Julie Moore," Theo yelled as Kori got into her car. "You could be Julie Moore's brother!"

Kori drove to work and took her place in the control room. Snorty, a man a little older than Kori who had worked at the station for nearly 16 years, was the evening switcher. He normally worked from 7:30 until sign-off, whatever time that might be. He was leaning back in his chair with both of his hands up over his head, playing with his hair, as was his habit.

"Hey, Snorty, how's it going?"

"Hey, Kori, bet you can't guess who they hired."

"They hired someone already?"

"Yeah, can you guess who it is?"

"How could I guess? I don't know any of those guys."

"You know one."

"No, I saw them today, and I don't know any of them."

"Yes, you do."

"Who?"

"Jim Smith."

"Who?"

"Jim Smith."

"Who's that?"

"You know, Jim Smith."

"No, I don't know Jim Smith."

"Oh, that's right! He left before you came! You were hired to replace him."

"Who is Jim Smith?"

"He had your position before you came here."

"Well, I don't know him."

"He hates you."

"What? Why? I haven't even met him."

"You met him today."

"I did?"

"Yeah, he left just a few minutes ago. He's starting tomorrow. He hates you." Snorty chuckled.

"What are you talking about? He doesn't even know me. Why would he hate me?"

"He just does. He thinks you stole his job."

"I didn't steal his job. He left and I just filled the opening. I didn't know him."

"Yeah, he left just before you came. He ran off to Iowa with Marissa when she got a job in a TV station there."

"Marissa Bumper? Do you mean the famous news beauty everyone used to talk about all the time? The one all the local stations were fighting to get to be news anchor, with the long hair and the long legs?"

"One and the same. Yep, they were lovers, Jim Smith and Marissa Bumper, hot and heavy, and when she got the job in Iowa, he quit his job and followed her there. I heard she got, like, double salary there."

"Did they get married?"

"I don't know. We never heard from them after they left."

"So why'd he come back? Is Marissa back?"

"I don't know. He didn't say. He just wanted to get his job back and now you have it. He's really upset."

"Well, he still got a job, one that pays the same as mine, and he works a normal work week, with much less stress than I have."

"Yeah, but he hates you."

"That is so unfair!"

"Life is unfair." Snorty snorted as he made that remark. Although he tended to snort often, that wasn't why they called him Snorty – his last name was Snortland, thus the nickname 'Snorty.'

"He doesn't even know me."

"He doesn't have to."

"What do you mean by that?"

"He can just hate you without knowing you."

"I think that's called being prejudice."

"I don't think so."

"Yes, it is! If he hates me and he hasn't even met me, that's prejudice, pre-judging, you know?"

"No, Jim's not the kind of guy to be prejudice."

The door to the control room flew open and slammed against the wall as Buddy burst into the room with a stack of papers.

"I need all these scores in," he demanded, shoving the papers at Kori.

"Okay," Kori said calmly. Snorty turned to face the wall of monitors so he could ignore the conversation.

"You better get them all in on time, before we go on. The baseball game will probably go into extra innings, but it might not, and in any case, I'll need those scores at the last minute, so you better be ready."

"Okay," Kori said again.

After Buddy left the room, Kori remarked, "I didn't know we were carrying a baseball game tonight."

"As soon as this program ends, we're joining the Twins' game in progress."

"They haven't won a game yet this year. Why does he think it would go into extra innings?"

"Ah, you know Buddy. He just wants to push you around, make you scared."

"I'm really scared," Kori said, smiling.

"You should be! You've seen his temper."

"Or lack of."

"That, too!"

Just then, Rob, the mellow weather man, glided into the control room.

"Looks like we have a storm front moving in," he said.

"We always have a front moving in," Snorty said. "When will we get the actual storm and not just the front?"

"Snorty, a front IS a storm. This is a storm front, a storm, and this one might be pretty bad, possibly some snow or ice," Rob warned. Kori wasn't surprised to hear about this type of weather in May – after all, this was North Dakota. The first year she lived here, the snow on the ground was still five feet high in May. "This just might hit us here," Rob said.

"So, are we doing a roll-over or a cut-in?" Kori asked.

"Here, type this in, we'll do a live update at the break." He handed her several sheets of paper. "I'm going to be using the map on camera two. Can you set up the camera? I haven't seen any of the floor crew here yet."

"Yeah, sure, do you have the map set up yet?" Kori asked.

"I'm going out there now to set it up. Snorty, what time is the break?"

"It starts in exactly seven minutes," Snorty said, checking the schedule.

"Will that give you enough time, Kori?" Rob asked.

"Let's set up the camera, then I'll get this typed in," she said.

"I can set it up for you, Rob, so Kori can type – if they go to break early, roll it, Kori, it's all set," Snorty said. "No, wait! The tapes are in, but you have to turn on the remote. I forgot, they were using the cart machine a few minutes ago."

"Yeah, sure," Kori said, as she began to type the weather warning graphics into the computer, while keeping an eye on the clock and an ear tuned to the program for the cue that the break was coming. She checked and double checked her spelling and glanced at the studio monitors to see that the cameras were set up and in place, and the studio lights had been turned on to the weather set where Rob was standing. Kori finished typing in the weather warning information, then she went to the tape room and turned on the cart machine. Snorty came back into the control room just as the network gave the closing announcement, and he dove to the switcher to start the machine and dissolve to the commercial that was on the tape. Kori had the graphics all ready to go as Snorty announced over the mic to the studio for Rob to stand by to go live. Kori saw Rob looking at the studio monitor, watching the commercial to see when it ended and Snorty would put him on the air. At the last second,

Rob remembered to clip on his mic and Kori dashed into the production room to turn on his audio, then she sprang back to her seat at the graphics computer as Snorty switched to the studio. Rob would have to watch his time, since there was no one in the studio to give him a signal; but if the local emergency weather warning went long, it would be understandable if they joined the network program in progress. Kori was so involved with the technical side of the production that she didn't pay any attention to what Rob was saying, or the warnings he was giving. They finished the weather cut-in just as the network was switching to the baseball game. Snorty joined the network and Kori gave him a station identification icon to superimpose over the video, since some type of station ID was required on the hour.

"What a team!" Rob said, as he returned to the control room. "I turned off the lights and cut the mic," he said. "Good job, guys; oh, sorry, Kori, I mean, guy and gal. Who needs a whole production team, anyway? Oh, Kori, can you type in this crawl? We need to run it every five minutes, Snorty."

"For how long?" Snorty asked.

"It's a 30-second crawl, repeat it twice, then keep running it every five minutes until we get an update. The storm is heading our way," Rob said. He glanced at the network monitor. "Twins winning?"

"Ha!" Snorty said. "What do you think? Actually, it's a tie, no score yet."

"What inning is this?" Rob asked.

"They just got started, they had a rain delay."

"So we're going on late?" Rob asked.

"Looks like it," Snorty said, "but who knows?"

"That's good and that's bad," Rob said.

"Why do you say that?" Kori asked.

"It's good because it'll give me more time to prepare for the newscast. I have an extra long weather segment tonight, and this will give me more chances to announce the storm, if we have a couple of extra breaks," Rob said

"So what's bad?" Kori asked.

"The storm is really bad, and I'm telling everyone to get home as soon as possible. We won't be able to get home as soon as possible, since we have to be here. We'll need to be here as long as the storm is bad, to keep people updated and keep warning them not to go out, and to list the closures for tomorrow."

"If the game goes late, I'll be here all night anyway," Snorty said. "I'll just ride out the storm here while I keep the station on the air."

"Well, some of us might want to get home safely," Kori said, as Rob returned to the newsroom to get the latest weather information.

"Why? You don't have anyone waiting at home for you," Snorty said.

"Tundra - my cat - is waiting for me!' Kori exclaimed. "She knows exactly what time to expect me. She'll panic if I'm late, especially if there's a storm. She'll really worry about me. Don't look at me like that. She's really smart. And anyway, I wouldn't talk if I were you. Who do you have waiting for you? Is your mother staying with you again? Or are you staying at your mother's place?"

"No, that's why I can stay here as long as I want. Nobody is worrying about me," Snorty boasted.

"Is that something to brag about?" Kori asked as she continued typing the news supers.

"I'm not bragging, just stating a fact," Snorty said. "Someday, the right girl will come along and we'll get married, but until then, I'm just going to enjoy being a happy bachelor, doing my own thing, whatever I want to do, and I'm not going to waste my money on dating and stuff. I'm not going to let some girl steal all my money or make me buy all kinds of junk for her. I'm going to find just the right girl who will want me for me, not for my money."

"What money?" Kori laughed.

"You just don't know how much I have," Snorty said, "and don't try to trick me into telling you. You're not my type."

"Thank God!" Kori said. "You have a type?"

"Yes, I have a type," Snorty said matter-of-factly. "And she's not like you."

"What do you mean, she's not like me?"

"You're too skinny," Snorty said. "I want a girl with some meat on her bones."

"Well, Mr. Snortland," Kori said, flattered that he said she was skinny, "in the first place, you're almost 40 years old. I think you better start looking for a woman, not a girl. Secondly, you've never even had a girlfriend. How do you even know what type you like, if you haven't ever had a relationship?"

"I know what I like and what I'm attracted to."

"You know WHAT you are attracted to? What is she, a thing, like your other gadgets? Just an item, merely an object? Are you going to buy her at Radio Shack?"

Snorty laughed and snorted. "I want a real woman, a decent woman, who looks and acts like a woman."

"Then you need to act like a decent man, I mean, at least ACT like one, if you can."

"Have you seen the new news reporter?" Snorty asked.

"Terry? The intern?"

"No, not him; the new reporter... the lady."

"Oh, you mean Rose?"

"Is that her name?"

"Rose isn't new. She's been doing the weekend news for a few months. I guess you wouldn't know because you never work on weekends."

"Rose, huh? Does she have a boyfriend?"

"Oh, you like her?"

"Shhh! I didn't say that."

"Ahhh, I see, *Rose* is your type."

"She looks nice and she smells good."

"Yeah, I noticed she always wears rose perfume."

"You never wear perfume."

"Not here! I work in a little box of a room with a bunch of sweaty guys! I don't want to choke you out with perfume. Oh, are you saying the perfume she's wearing makes her your type?"

"I didn't say that."

"I see, it's not just her perfume, but the way she looks and the way she dresses?"

"She looks pretty."

"She has to look pretty, she's on TV."

As if summoned, Rose came into the control room carrying several news tapes. She looked from Kori to Snorty as they looked at her, smiling.

"What?" Rose asked. "What are you looking at? Did I spill something on my blouse?"

"No," Kori said. "We were just joking around."

"About what?" Rose asked.

"Nothing important," Snorty said.

"Snorty was just explaining--" Kori began.

"I was just talking to Kori," Snorty said guiltily.

"Were you telling her a dirty joke?" Rose asked.

"No!" Snorty said, his face turning bright red. He turned away from Rose, toward the wall of monitors, and began to study them intently.

"Well, here are the tapes for the ten o'clock," she said, nodding her head as if she didn't believe him. "Most of them have been cut down so we can spend as much time as we need on the weather. Have you been running the crawl? I didn't see it from the newsroom monitor."

"We're just about to run it now," Kori said, calling up the crawl onto her preview monitor. "Ready, Snorty?"

"Give it to me," he said. "Okay, we're running it now."

"Great, I'll let Rob know," Rose said. "Every five minutes, right?"

"Yes, ma'am," Snorty said, giggling.

"He's going to want to go live again at the next local break," Rose said.

"No problem, we've got it," Kori said.

"What time is the next break?" Rose asked.

"You better set him up out there now," Snorty said. "They are supposed to go to break after the next inning, but that guy got injured, so this inning is stretching out. They could go at any time. I'm just listening for the cue."

"Then you better stop telling dirty jokes and start paying more attention to the game," Rose warned with a smile.

"Yes, ma'am," Snorty said with a huge grin, as Rose left the control room. Rose was clearly in a league way above anything Snorty could ever approach, but Kori was amused by his interest in her. She hadn't ever seen Snorty noticing anyone before; he was generally a loner who just did his job, kind of like Kori, only completely different; because he was really weird and he looked as if he only washed his hair once a month. Kori didn't have a problem with Snorty. They worked well together and they respected each other, but of all the single guys at the station, Snorty was at the bottom of the list of anyone who could ever attract her. Seven single

27

guys worked in the production department: Don was cute but crazy and Kori had heard he was a heavy drinker at parties; Sandy was good-looking and very nice but kind of slow; Brad was nice but Kori suspected he had a substance abuse problem; Tom was very smart and quite shy, and no one else at the station liked him due to his completely passive personality; Big Jeff was really young, he was handsome and he knew it; Dennis was short and bald and he was always a nervous wreck; and then there was Snorty, the muscular bone-head.   Barry was engaged, so he didn't count as one of the single guys, and the rest of the men in the production crew were all married.   In   the   news   department,   only   the   second-string sportscaster, Danny, was single, and he was a total sports head who didn't know a single thing outside of the sports field, and in the engineering department, all the guys were married.

Buddy slammed the door against the wall as he came into the control room again.

"I've got all these scores, you need to get them in before the news," he demanded.

"Okay," Kori replied.

"I can't believe this is only the second inning!" Buddy shouted. "But that gives me more time to get everything together – and you should have plenty of time to get all that in. You will get it all in, right?" he said as he banged the door against the wall again on his way out of the control room, not waiting for her reply.

"Yes," Kori said. She didn't like talking to Buddy since he was so overbearing, so she always responded with a brief and positive answer so he would leave the room as soon as possible. They had worked together for more than five years, and she doubted that he knew her name. To him, she was just part of the machinery at the station, something to be used, and cursed when it didn't work correctly, or the way he thought it should work. She didn't care; he was like all the jocks from high school with their heads so high in the sports clouds they didn't know real life and real people existed outside the sports arena. Kori couldn't understand why Maureen had married him. Kori loved Maureen. She was so nice and so friendly, and she didn't really have an interest in sports. The rumor was that Maureen and Buddy had been high school sweethearts, but they were a very odd match. It was obvious why Buddy had been attracted to beautiful and kind Maureen, but nobody had any idea what Maureen could possibly see in Buddy.

During the break, they did the live weather warning. Then Kori finished typing in all the news supers and the sports scores. The baseball game was going long, but they were obligated to stay with the network programming until the game ended, so Rob did several more weather warning updates and Kori ran the severe weather warning crawl every five minutes.

Working at the TV station was exciting, but by 11:30, Kori was beginning to get really sleepy. The news should have ended an hour ago, and it hadn't even started yet. The baseball game was going into extra innings, still with no score. Because of the extra-long game and the severe weather warnings, Kori was going to get some extra overtime this week. She already was scheduled to work on Saturday to cover for one of the weekend switchers, so these extra late night hours would add a nice little amount to her paycheck.

"It must be getting pretty bad out there," Snorty commented, as Rob entered the control room with another weather update for Kori to type into the computer.

"This is North Dakota. The weather is always bad," Kori said.

"Not always," Snorty protested.

"Almost always. We had snow just two weeks ago. Take a look at these national temps. Where I'm from, in Washington state, it was 85 degrees today. Here, we are having the worst weather in the country," Kori said.

"Not the worst, look at northern Minnesota," Rob said. "They already have three inches of ice AND the wind is blowing 80 miles an hour."

"And look at Alaska," Snorty said. "They still have six feet of snow in some areas."

"Rob, how can you do the weather, day after day, when it's always so bad?" Kori asked. "I mean, isn't it hard? It must be depressing, for you and for the viewers, to hear it's going to be so cold, with so much snow, for so much of the year."

"The trick is," Rob said, bending toward Kori, as if he were telling her a secret, "to always point out somewhere where the weather is worse than ours. That way, people at home see that and say to themselves, 'At least I'm not there. Look how bad it is there.' Like tonight, I'll talk about northern Minnesota and Alaska, and then

I'll make a comment about how the people in Florida are suffering in all that humidity. The people who live here will be glad to know that the ice storm is passing through our area and the conditions are worse in other areas. And also, in our area, the weather is predictable. We can see the storms coming, so we can warn the viewers. Tonight, everyone is prepared for an ice storm. I would never want to do the weather in the Pacific Northwest. It is so unpredictable with all those mountains. A storm can be coming straight at Portland or Seattle, and then suddenly just turn and go offshore, or the skies can be perfectly clear, then the clouds come out of nowhere and dump a load of rain on the whole area. Look at the jet stream in that area tonight. They were all set to have clear weather, then that cold air from Alaska met with the warm air from Hawaii, and they got a huge amount of rain."

Rain sounded kind of nice to Kori, after the months of snow and ice they had been experiencing in North Dakota. After all, the ice and snow on the roads had just finally melted after being frozen solid since November. She thought of the joke about the four seasons in North Dakota: snow, snow, snow and road repair. She smiled to herself, even though it was so true, it wasn't really funny.

Kori smiled at Rob. "Well, you have a really good attitude about it," she said.

"Attitude is everything," Rob said.

Kori nodded, although she had no idea what he meant by that remark.

Finally, at 12:50, the baseball game ended and the news started. Everybody was feeling tired and goofy, and the news was much more relaxed than usual, since tonight, everyone had time to finish everything before the news started. The ice storm was beginning to hit their area and just four people from the news team – the four who were on air – were the only members of the news team still at the station.

As soon as the news ended, Rob brought several more severe weather warnings for Kori to type, to be crawled across the screen for the next couple of hours. The rest of the production crew went home, along with the rest of the news team. Kori and Snorty were the only two people left at the station. Kori always had a few things to do after the rest of the crew left, while Snorty set up everything he had to do to finish out the broadcasting day. Kori was getting so tired, she was almost giddy, laughing to herself for no reason at all. Her thoughts seemed to be so funny; then her feet started bothering each other. Her right foot couldn't stand for her left foot to be touching it. She giggled as she corrected a silly spelling error that would never be seen by the public. It was nearly two in the morning. She needed to get home and go to bed.

"Okay, that about does it," Kori told Snorty. "Are you all set? Can I go now?"

"Yep," Snorty said. "Be careful out there."

"I only have to go a few blocks," Kori said.

"But the roads might be pretty icy out there," Snorty warned.

"I know! We've been doing weather warnings for the past five hours."

"I'm just saying to be careful."

"And I'm just saying I will be careful."

"Okay, then."

"Okay, then."

"Bye."

"Good night."

"Good morning!"

"Yeah, that's what I meant."

CHAPTER 5

Kori let herself out through the back door of the TV station. The instant her shoe touched the parking lot, both of her feet flew straight out in front of her, and she thumped onto her bottom on the ground. As her eyes adjusted to the dark, she could see that everything was coated with at least an inch of ice. She pulled herself to her feet and slowly scooted across the parking lot to her car. She grabbed onto the side mirror as she almost fell again, and she took her key out of her pocket. She looked at the car door and realized it would be impossible to put the key in the lock – it was deep below the surface of the ice. She tried it anyway, and it was as if she were trying to just put the key anywhere into the car body. She attempted to chip away some of the ice, but with no success. It was too thick.

She slowly inched her feet around to the back of her car, leaning against it, trying to grip it, so she wouldn't fall again, thinking maybe she could put the key into the lock on the hatchback. She found an even larger mound of ice covering that lock. She thought about her options. She could walk – or slide – home from the station and leave her car there, but the road was covered with ice and she was freezing already. She hadn't worn a heavy enough coat to be outside for very long in this suddenly extremely cold weather. She could stay at the station, but where would she sleep? Could she relax enough to sleep on the couch in the front reception room? No, she couldn't even go to sleep unless she took out her contacts, and she didn't have her contact case with her. She could not sleep while she was wearing her contacts – she couldn't fall asleep without removing them – so if she stayed here, she wouldn't be to able go to sleep.

Kori didn't know what to do, but she knew she couldn't stay outside and freeze any longer. She looked at the back door of the station, seemingly miles away, and began scooting toward it so she could go back into its welcoming warmth and decide what to do. After falling two more times, she finally made it to the door without having to crawl across the ice. She found that the lock on the station door was coated with ice, so she couldn't use her key here either. She reached for the doorbell, which was used primarily by delivery persons, and she saw the doorbell was also covered with an inch of ice. She couldn't even ring the bell. She pounded with her bare hand on the frozen surface of the door, hoping by some miracle Snorty would hear her. Why had she chosen to be one of the only people in the country without a cell phone? She really should carry one for emergencies – but then, her mom's suggestion for her to keep one in her car wouldn't do her any good now, would it? Although her brain was frozen by now and she couldn't think, her instincts took control of her and told her to bang on the slab of ice, usually called a door, with her keys.

After the longest minute in the history of the world, Snorty opened the door.

"Are you still here?" Snorty asked.

"No, I left fifteen minutes ago."

"That's what I thought. Why'd you come back?"

"Let me in! It's below freezing out here!"

"What are you doing? I thought you were going home."

"What am I NOT doing? Going home! My car is coated with a thick layer of ice and I can't get in it!"

"What are you going to do?" he asked, finally opening the door wide enough for her to enter the warm building. Her teeth were chattering.

"I don't know. I can't stay here – I need to get home and take out my contacts. I've had them in for more than 20 hours and my eyes are killing me."

"I thought you were getting laser surgery."

"I've been thinking about it but I haven't done it yet."

"Well, maybe you should get it."

"Maybe I should! But not tonight! I need to get home!"

"What are you going to do?"

"I don't know! Boiling water? Would that work?"

"Where are you going to get boiling water?"

"The microwave in Gary's office?"

"It's broken, hasn't worked for about two months. He's going to get a new one."

"What about the coffee pot where the front office staff makes their coffee? I could boil some water and then pour it on the door lock."

"You don't want to do that, because even if you can get it to thaw enough to get your key in the lock, you won't be able to open it tomorrow, or as long as it stays below freezing, because the water will get inside the lock and it will really freeze up. That happened to my mom before."

"Why do people live in this place where the climate is unfit for humans to live?" Kori demanded. "Okay, how about a lighter? I could heat up the key and then maybe melt enough around the lock to put in the key. Do you have a lighter?"

"A lighter?"

"Yeah, a cigarette lighter."

"No, you know I don't smoke! It's a disgusting habit! I would never carry anything associated with cigarettes."

"Me neither, but I thought maybe... I know! We can look in some of the front offices, maybe someone has one in their desk."

"Do you have a key to those offices?"

"Oh, no, are they locked? Why is everything locked tonight? Why am I locked out of everything tonight? What can I do? Maybe I'll just go sit in Maureen's comfy chair." Maureen had brought a comfortable chair for her desk because she had been so uncomfortable with all the weight she had gained during her pregnancy.

"The newsroom is locked."

"What? Why do they lock the newsroom? You're the only one here. Don't they trust you?"

"It's not because of me."

"Well, you're no help at all," Kori said, defeated.

"I have a blowtorch in my truck," Snorty said.

"A blowtorch? What's that?"

"It shoots fire. We could use it to thaw your lock."

"YOU could use it to thaw my lock? Why didn't you say something?"

"I did," he said, laughing.

"Before now!" Kori said, relieved. She WOULD get home tonight, or, this morning. As quickly as her hopes were raised, her balloon burst. "It's in your truck? How can you open your truck? It's just as frozen as my car."

"I never lock it," Snorty said. "I can't believe you lock your car. No one does around here."

"Yeah, I know, I get teased all the time. I'm the only one in this state who locks my car. It's a habit, even after living in this nice, safe community all these years. I automatically lock my car doors, without even thinking about it."

"After this next break that's coming up, I'll go out and get my blowtorch, and we can see if we can get into your car. Good thing I have a blowtorch."

The name 'blowtorch' made it sound like a very scary tool, but Kori figured if Snorty had one, he must know how to use it.

"Why do you have a blowtorch, anyway?" Kori asked.

"Just in case I need it, like tonight," he explained.

"What do you use it for?"

"Getting into cars that are frozen over with ice," he giggled.

"Really? You had to do that before?"

"No, this is the first time I've had to do that. Hold on a minute," he said, going over to the master control switcher. He ran the commercial break, then he put on his big, green, heavy coat with the fur-lined hood.

"Oh, you might want to prop open the door," Kori warned. "The lock is frozen on the outside and you won't be able to get your key within an inch of it."

Snorty put a door-stopper under the door and Kori followed him out to the parking lot. The temperature must have dropped another ten degrees, and Kori was instantly chilled to her bones. She began to shiver as they inched their way across the iced-over pavement to Snorty's pickup truck, which had a cover over the back. He lifted open the door on the back and pulled out a large contraption. Kori followed him, again sliding, over to her little car. Snorty fiddled with some knobs and adjustments, then he turned a switch, and a flame about six inches long shot out of the end of the blowtorch. He put it near the lock on the driver's door, and the ice melted very quickly. He stepped away from the car and turned off the blowtorch.

Kori was able to put her key in the lock, but it wouldn't turn! The mechanism inside was frozen. She tried to turn it, but she was afraid the key would break off in the lock, so she pulled it out and shook her head. She couldn't say anything – her teeth were chattering too much. She motioned with her hand for him to go to the hatchback and she scooted to the back of the car and pointed at the lock. Again, Snorty turned on the blowtorch and melted the ice from the lock on the hatchback, then he turned off the blowtorch. Kori tried her key. It turned! She nodded her head at Snorty and tried to lift open the hatchback. It was frozen shut! She pulled and pulled, but it wouldn't move.

Snorty slid over to the hatchback and set the blowtorch on the ground. He pulled on the handle and Kori could hear a crackling sound as the ice began to crack around the edges of the hatchback. He pulled a second time, and the hatchback door came open. Kori nodded and climbed into the car through the hatchback. The back door slammed shut. The air inside the car was so still and cold as she climbed across the back seat and into the driver's seat. She put the key in the ignition and she was so thankful when the car started on the first turn of the key. She tried to see if Snorty was still near the car, or if he had made it back to the station, but since the windows were coated with ice and the night was so dark, she couldn't see a thing outside the car. Inside the car, all she could see was her breath and the dim glow of the indicator lights in her dashboard. She thought about turning on her windshield wipers, but she realized they would be coated with ice also. She turned on the defroster to the highest setting and cringed when the cold air bounced off the window and onto her face. She dared not smile or even open her mouth – if she did, she knew the freezing air would go right to her gold filling, and that would really hurt.

She tried to unlock the driver's door and she discovered it was frozen from in here, too. She couldn't open the door without unlocking it. She thought that the whole insides of her door must be frozen, between the vinyl inside and the metal outside of the car door. Well, she had a good heater in the car and it would be warm in no time. The defroster had already melted two holes in the ice on the windshield that were almost an inch in diameter. She gave the car some gas and she was glad she always kept the tank nearly full, remembering the advice of her Uncle Andy, "It's just as easy to keep the top half of the tank full as it is to keep the bottom half full."

Kori switched on the radio but she couldn't find a station on the air. She thought that was rather odd, then she figured that most people had gone home because of the storm, even the ones who worked at the radio stations. She thought about the fact that her car was probably the only one in town that still had just a radio and cassette tape player, and no CD player; she knew she couldn't play a frozen tape in a frozen tape deck. She rubbed her hands together and wondered why she had removed her gloves from the glove

36

compartment. She sat on her hands in an effort to keep them warm as she stared at the little melted holes in the ice on the windshield, now nearly two inches wide. She bent down so she could see through the holes. She figured she would be able to see enough to drive in just a few minutes. After all, she only had to go a few blocks, and she doubted that she would meet anyone else on the road.

She waited about ten more minutes, put the car in reverse, stepped on the gas pedal – and the car didn't move. The car was frozen to the parking lot! The engine whined but the wheels didn't turn! She pressed harder on the gas pedal, and finally the wheels spun. The car slid slowly across the icy parking lot. She stepped on the brake, at the same time realizing the brakes would be no good on ice, so she let her foot off the brake pedal and the car slid to a stop. She would be driving home on a giant ice rink.

She could do this. She just had to go very slowly. She put the car in drive and eased very slowly on the gas pedal. The car moved forward very slowly. She began to drive out of the parking lot and noticed the speedometer was not even registering any speed. She figured that even if she went only one mile per hour, she would be home in about twenty minutes, and now that the inside of the car was no longer freezing, she could stand it. She was going to make it home. She smiled to herself, thinking how funny it would be if Theo were standing on his balcony to greet her when she got home.

She inched the car along on the icy, barren streets. She didn't see another car on the road, nor did she see any lights in any of the homes she passed. She hoped the electricity was still working in this area. After what seemed like an hour in the car, she turned into her own parking lot and parked the car. When she reached to unlock the door, she discovered that the lock was still frozen! She couldn't open the door! She would have to climb out through the hatchback. Oh, no, that was a bad idea, because the hatchback door only opened from the outside!

By now the windows were nearly clear and she could see that there was not a soul around who could open the hatchback for her. Although she had only turned off the car and the heat a moment ago, the inside of the car was already very cold. Maybe she could climb out the window. She tried to turn the handle, but the window was frozen shut, the handle wouldn't turn. She started the car again and turned the heat on high.

Kori thought about the family who had died in the car this past winter when they had a flat tire and waited for help inside the car with the heater going. Was she going to die tonight? Why didn't she have a cell phone so she could call for help? Who would she call? She could call her parents, who lived 1200 miles to the west, and tell them goodbye... or her dad would give her a great idea, and she would then be able to get out of the car. What would he say? Honk the horn!

She pushed the horn button on the steering wheel and nothing happened. She remembered that in the winter, her horn never worked. Even when the weather was warm and the horn did work, it wasn't very loud. At its loudest, her horn wouldn't be able to awaken a sleeping neighbor from the parking lot. When she had purchased her car, she had been living in Washington state. This car had not been made to stay for an extended period of time in such cold weather. She remembered when she first moved here and she thought it was the strangest thing when a lady told her that she always plugged in her car during the winter nights. Then she noticed electrical cords hanging out through the grills of all the cars around here. She later learned the cars that had been purchased here had something called 'block heaters' that plugged in to an outlet. The heaters kept the car engines warm in the sub-zero weather. Whoever had invented that had really had a good idea - good for the people who had purchased a car with a block heater. Kori never thought she needed one, because her little Honda always started, even in the coldest weather. Besides, was she going to live in this climate for the rest of her life? She was really different from the people who were raised here – she knew she could move to a warmer climate some day, but the Dakotans never seemed to even consider the idea of leaving this area. They didn't seem to know they could choose not to live in this extremely cold climate.

Why had she stayed here for so many years? She loved her job and the friendly people here. She did not like the weather, but she wasn't really outside in the weather very much; she spent most of her life inside buildings, either at work or in her apartment. Her apartment was well insulated, so it was very cozy and warm when

38

the weather was cold, and it was nice and cool during the short season when the weather was hot.

She longed to be inside her cozy apartment right now. She searched in vain for anybody who could open the hatchback and let her out of her car. She had been awake for nearly twenty-four hours. Her eyes were incredibly dry and irritated by her contacts. Every blink of her eyelids was torturing her eyes. She tried to not blink very often, to minimize the pain her eyes were feeling, but that seemed to make her eyes feel even more dry than they had been, and the dryness made her more desperate to blink them. She wanted to take out her contacts and close her eyes in sleep! How much longer did she have to wait in this car, before she could get out and go inside the apartment that was calling to her?

Kori thought about Tundra. She would be sleeping on Kori's pillow, waiting for her to come home. As soon as Kori came into the bedroom, Tundra would look up at her sleepily, with smiling eyes, give a quick lick to a paw or her chest, and wait for Kori to put her head on the pillow beside her. Then Tundra would move closer, begin purring loudly, and fall asleep with her head resting on Kori's head. Kori often thought about how she was everything to Tundra, from provider to companion to petting machine to pillow. Kori would so love to just bury her fingers – or even her face – in Tundra's silky fur right now, and to be able to feel the vibration of her purring. What would Tundra do if she died out here? Who would take care of her? Tundra was more than twelve years old. She would be put to sleep if someone didn't adopt her – and she had always been so scared of other people. She was not really friendly, so who would want to rescue her? Kori had to get out of this car, for Tundra's sake, if for no other reason.

She half-heartedly tried the lock again and was surprised that it moved! She was now able to unlock the car door! She could get out of the car now! She pushed on the door, which was frozen shut. She turned sideways in her seat so she could break the seal of ice by pushing the door with her feet. After several pushes, she finally was able to open the door! She didn't want to even think about how long the lock had been thawed. She turned off the engine. She stepped out of the car and closed the door, and she did not lock it, for the first time since she had bought it twelve years ago, the day before she got Tundra. She felt so uneasy about leaving her car unlocked, feeling as if she were somehow undone or exposed, but she forced herself to walk – or slide – up the steps, holding the icy railing and scoot along the icy sidewalk toward the apartment building. After a few steps on the sidewalk, she had a brainstorm – she should be walking on the grass, because although it was also frozen under more than an inch of ice, she would be able to get some traction and she could move a bit faster toward the door.

She finally made it to the outer door of the apartment building, opened the door, and stepped inside the foyer and unlocked the inside door. When she entered the hallway, she realized that she hadn't been taking any deep breaths, because the air outside was so cold. She also noticed her hands were about to freeze off the end of her arms. They were burning from the heat of the air inside the building. Her keys fell from her hand and as she bent over to get them, she couldn't move her fingers. She could have frostbite on her fingers!

Her mind flashed back to a time shortly after she had moved here, during the winter Rob had said was the coldest winter they had had in a hundred years, when she was at the grocery store. She was waiting in the check-out line when a little boy came in the door, crying, to a lady who was in line in front of Kori. He held out his bare hands to her, unable to speak, still crying. His hands were so red. The lady, who may have been his mother, didn't say a thing. She gently took his hands in her own, and then, she lifted up her coat and sweater to expose her skin around her middle. She put his hands on her bare stomach, under her clothes, and she pulled the sweater and coat over his hands and held them close to her. Kori had gasped at the thought of those cold hands on her bare body, but the lady must have had some experience with this method of warming hands, for she stood there for a few minutes to allow the boy's hands to get warm from the warmth of her body.

Kori knew now that she would not be able to pick up her keys until her fingers could function, so she slipped her hands under her own shirt and wrapped her arms around her body. Her fingers felt as if they were on fire. Her midriff felt as if she had just put some ice cubes under her shirt. She suddenly felt as if she were going to faint. She wanted to sit on the steps, but they were so far from her, so she let herself collapse cross-legged onto the floor. Her head was spinning and pounding, she couldn't stand her frozen hands touching herself; she was exhausted. Where was her nosy neighbor, Theo, now, or anybody who could help her? The managers, a married couple, lived at the far end of the hall, but they would be asleep now, along with everyone else in the building.

Kori was okay sitting on the floor. She just needed a few minutes to thaw, to get warm, to rest; but she couldn't go to sleep here, because she still had to take out her contacts before she could close her eyes! She couldn't let herself relax here, in the hallway. She remembered to breathe, and a few minutes later, she was able to feel her fingers begin to approach some resemblance of being normal again. She took out her right hand and slowly moved her fingers. Her fingers felt as if they were twice their regular size, but they didn't look puffy or unusual. Kori was always a little irritated when she felt pain in her body but could see nothing out of the ordinary in that area. When something hurt, she wanted some type of physical evidence. Now she had none. She convinced herself that her hands were back to their normal state and she reached for her keys. She was able to grab them. She pulled herself to her feet and somehow she made it to her apartment.

She opened the door and headed straight for the bathroom to remove her contacts. She then brushed her teeth with her eyes closed and made a beeline for her bed. Tundra was waiting for her on the pillow, and Kori snuggled in close to her, fast asleep before she even felt Tundra's head on hers.

CHAPTER 6

Kori slammed the apartment door and rushed down the stairs as quickly as possible, taking two steps at a time. Her heart was pounding so hard in her chest, it felt as if her heart were going to burst through her rib cage. Her mouth was so dry, it was painful to inhale, but she had to hurry and get far away from this place. She was so relieved that she didn't meet anyone in the stairwell, no one who could be a witness that she had been here.

She pulled her hood over her head as she stepped out of the building and into the dark of the night. She was going to get away from here, she was going to get away with her crime. How could she have done it? She had murdered someone! She had taken a person's life! She had ended a life, a life that only God could create. No one could ever know of this hideous deed; but she would have to carry this burden of guilt, secret guilt, for the rest of her life. She could never tell anyone about it. What would people think about her if they knew she was a murderer? Oh, what was she thinking? If she ever told anybody, she would be arrested and go to jail for the rest of her life! She could never tell anybody! She could never admit committing this horrible crime to anyone!

Now she had to get as far from the crime scene as she could, as quickly as possible. She had to get home to her own bed and go to sleep and forget this had ever happened. What exactly had happened? She had killed someone! However, if no one ever discovered what she had done, if she could keep it to herself for the rest of her life, she could go on with her life as if nothing had happened, as if she were not guilty. She could forget about it and go on with her life.

Where did she get that idea? She could never forget that she had killed someone. She had ended a life. A person had been living, alive, and she had stopped it! She had no right to end another person's life! She was guilty, but she would never be able to admit it to anyone. She had become the worst of criminals. She made a promise to herself that she would never again commit a crime; she wouldn't even jaywalk. She would live the rest of her life as a saint, never so much as even thinking an evil thought about anyone. She would change her life, starting from this moment, and she would never turn back into the evil person she had been, the wicked murderer who had ended a person's life.

She rounded the corner from the alley and was relieved to see the streets were deserted. She would get away from this part of town and she would never return to this vicinity. She had no reason to be here: she had lived her entire life without coming here until tonight, so she could live the rest of her life avoiding this area. She didn't need to be here ever again. She would get away from here and no one would ever know she had been here, and she herself would forget about it. Yes, it was fresh in her memory now; it had just happened; but, like all other memories, it would eventually fade and one day she would question if it really happened or not. If she never spoke about it to anyone, if she never admitted it even to herself, maybe it didn't really happen.

It really did happen. She knew she would never be free of the burden of guilt. She continued to walk as quickly as she could down one street, and then another. She was still in an unfamiliar area of town. Her legs began to ache, and she was beginning to get rather warm. She had to get away from this area! She still hadn't seen anyone on the streets, but she couldn't see anybody, or, actually, nobody could see her. She couldn't be seen in this area so nobody could connect her with the murder.

Why had she done it? She had taken a life, stopped a life, snuffed out the life of a living being, and she had no power to give life. She had always thought of herself as a giver – now she had become a taker. Why couldn't she walk any faster? How far was she from her own part of town? She was exhausted! She pulled one heavy foot, then the other, forcing herself to keep moving.

The scenery began to blend with something familiar. What was that, in the darkness, blending with the brick buildings? It looked like a window, with curtains, dark gray and black... oh, it was her window in her room! She was asleep; no, she was beginning to awaken. She was at home! The murder was not real! It was only a dream, a nightmare! She really did not kill anyone! She had never actually killed a person! What a relief! That huge burden of guilt was not her burden! She was free to be herself again, a regular person. She was not a person carrying a horrible secret for the rest of her life!

She couldn't go back to sleep now. She could not return to that nightmare. She looked at the clock. Only four minutes had passed since she had fallen asleep. She was so tired, so sleepy, but she could not let herself go back to sleep.

CHAPTER 7

Kori reached for the remote control and turned on the TV in her room. Her body was too tired to move, so maybe she could just keep her mind awake while she watched a program on TV. She flipped through the stations to find something interesting on cable. Interesting programs seemed to be more and more rare these days. She stopped on a station that had a movie. Was that Mandy Moore? She liked Mandy Moore. No, maybe it was Anne Hathaway. She liked Anne Hathaway too. Maybe it wasn't either one of them, but it was somebody attractive and young, with pretty, full lips. Whoever she was, she was entering school, a high school or college, with a group of other students and it seemed to be the first day of school. Kori turned up the volume on the TV so she could hear it.

The actress – the Anne/Mandy look-alike – walked up the steps with her head down, not too happy to be there, carrying her books as if they were full of lead. Kori noticed a huge cross on the wall and thought this must be a Catholic school or a Christian school. A few adults passed the young lady, none of them dressed as nuns or priests, so Kori figured it was a Christian school.

"Hey," a cute boy said to her, "are you new here?"

She smiled at the boy and nodded, and she looked more like Anne Hathaway.

"Well, I'm Jason," the boy said, tossing his blond hair. "What's your name?"

"Mandy," she said softly.

Kori decided she couldn't be Mandy Moore, because she didn't think Mandy Moore would play a girl named Mandy.

"Well, maybe we'll have some classes together," Jason said. "Who do you have for homeroom?"

"Um, let me see," Mandy said, pulling a piece of paper out of one of her books. "I have Mr. La—Riv—er—"

"LaRiviere?" Jason asked. "Oh, I knew I shouldn't have transferred out of that class! You're gonna love him! He's really nice. He's a great guy, funny, a real cool dude."

Did people actually talk like that, Kori wondered, using phrases like 'cool dude?' She thought they looked a little too old to be in high school, but colleges didn't have a homeroom, did they? Maybe this was an old movie; however, it didn't matter when the movie was made, as long as it could keep her awake and away from her hideous dreams.

"Great," Mandy said.

"I gotta go, my class is way across campus, but maybe I'll see you - no, I WILL definitely see you later," Jason said with a huge smile. His teeth were so bright white they were hurting Kori's eyes. She wanted to turn down the contrast on her TV, but since he quickly left the scene, she decided to leave it as it was.

Mandy turned a corner, her head still facing the floor, and she nearly ran into an elderly woman standing in the hallway. She slowly raised her head, examining the woman, all the way from her sports shoes, to her white nylons, to her long brown and beige dress to her face, which revealed a smiling mouth and frowning brow, to her gray curls which stuck out from beneath her funny brown hat.

"You must be Mandy," the woman said. Mandy looked like she was afraid of her.

"Yes, I am," Mandy answered meekly.

"Well, Mandy, normally we don't accept heathens here," the woman said, "but we made an exception in your case, because of your Aunt June. I can see, with some hard work from both sides, we can get you converted, and before long, you will be happy to proclaim Jesus Christ as your Lord and Savior, and, oh, what a day of rejoicing that will be! You will no longer be walking these halls with your head hanging down! You will be standing tall, and proud to be a Christian!"

Mandy looked very skeptical, as if she didn't believe the woman. Or perhaps, like Kori, she didn't understand what the woman meant. What did it mean to be converted? Why would she want to be converted? What would she become once she was converted? If she were a heathen, would she be converted into a non-heathen? What was a heathen, anyway?

Mandy adjusted her books and was about to walk away from the woman when the woman warned her, "You might think you are getting away with your sins. You might think you are hiding your sins and your sinful ways, but your sins are as bright as day in front of God, and you can't hide anything from Him. Don't be deceived – God is not mocked, and whatever you sow, that is what you will reap."

46

"I'm not sewing anything," Mandy said.

"Oh, yes, you are."

"I'll do my best," Mandy said, in her own defense.

"Your best isn't good enough for God!" the woman shouted. "The righteousness of man is as filthy rags before God!"

Mandy wrinkled her nose and made a face of disgust. "You don't want me to do my best?"

"Don't you dare mock God!"

"I'm not mocking Him!"

"Oh, my young child, you have no idea how far you are from God right now, but Jesus is just standing at the door and knocking!" the woman said. "Aren't you going to open up and let Him in?"

"What door?"

"Don't you make fun of me!"

"Really, I have no idea what you are talking about," Mandy said, slowly shaking her head. Kori nodded in agreement. That woman seemed to be really crazy.

"Don't let the ruler of this world, the prince of the air, the deceiver of mankind, pull the wool over your eyes!" the woman insisted.

"What are you talking about?" Mandy asked. Kori thought that was an excellent question. Wasn't God the ruler of the world?

"Don't try to play dumb with me!" the woman shouted. "I'm talking about you!"

"I'm the prince of the air?" Mandy asked. "How can I be a prince?"

"Don't you get smart with me, young lady!" the elderly woman said. "I am going to be watching you, and you are not going to get away with anything! Heaven forbid! You will not be able to plant seeds of doubt! You will not be able to turn our young men away from the Lord! You will not bring the world into our body of believers!"

"Really, I still don't know what you are talking about," Mandy said.

"Are you telling me that you are spiritually DEAD?" the woman asked.

"No, I'm telling you that I have no idea what you mean," Mandy said, clearly confused.

"The Spirit of God is speaking to you!" the woman shouted. "Open up your spiritual eyes and listen to Him!"

"How can I listen with my eyes?"

"Young lady, listen to Him!"

"I'm sorry, but the only one I can hear right now is you, shouting at me," Mandy said, "and I'm about to be late for class, so if you will please excuse me…"

"There's no excuse! I'm warning you, you are not going to get away with anything!"

"I don't want to get away with anything."

"You won't!"

Kori changed the channel. A man in a white coat, who looked like a scientist, was standing in front of a big chalkboard holding a gallon jug of water.

"Water," he said, "is the answer to all our problems. Is your skin too dry? There's no need to use moisturizer or lotions. Forget about expensive skin treatments. Just drink more water." He removed the cap from the jug of water and took a drink, a big, noisy gulp. "You need to moisturize your body from the inside, not the outside. Putting something on your skin only blocks your pores and makes your skin less able to eliminate toxins from your body."

Kori began to get thirsty, but her body was too tired to get out of bed to get a glass of water.

"Are your lips too dry? You could spend a lot of money on special lip balms and waxy coatings, but what you really need is more water." He took another big gulp from the jug.

"Do you have too many wrinkles? Does your face look like a relief map? Water is the answer! Not on the outside, but inside! Drink more water!" He took a small sip of water.

"How many people spend a lot of money to try to make the outside of their bodies look younger, money spent on salves, lotions, conditioners, creams, butters, and moisturizers? How much money did you spend last year, or last month, or even last week, on something to add moisture to the outside of your body? Were you like the millions of Americans who spent thousands of dollars on something you hoped would help you to look younger?" He took another sip of water from the jug.

"Have you ever left a grape or an apple or a plum or an orange or tomato just sitting out on the counter and then gone on vacation?

What happens to that piece of fruit? It dries up! What does that mean? These fruits are made up mostly of water. It's not the sun that dries them up and leaves them lifeless; it's the loss of water. The water that was inside the fruit evaporates and the piece of fruit is left wrinkled, a prune, a raisin, a useless, dried-up orange, all because it lost its water. Would you spread a lotion or a moisturizer on a raisin to restore its youthful, grape-like qualities? No, you wouldn't! Are people any different from fruit?"

Kori questioned that question: of course, people are different from fruit! This guy was kind of fruity, though, and he was kind of funny. Was he being serious or was this a comedy program? He was kind of handsome, he seemed sincere, and he had some good points. He looked like a doctor.

"A little bit of water does a little bit of good for your body," he said. "Now, it's a scientific fact that a lack of water causes a myriad of problems in the human body. Do you realize that the older you get, the more dehydrated your body becomes? We start out in liquid, in the womb, and when we are born, we have the most beautiful skin. Baby skin is not beautiful because it's so new and fresh, it's beautiful because it's fully hydrated." He drank more of the water. Kori felt the urge to go to the bathroom just because he was drinking so much water.

"We start out in life with the right amount of water. Our bodies are functioning well. We don't have any of the diseases of older people. Look at a baby. He has no wrinkles. He's fully hydrated. We come into the world like that. Then, over the years, as we decrease our water intake and are drinking so much less water than we need, our bodies learn to function with an insufficient amount of water. Think of the diseases that could be avoided completely if everyone would just drink as much water as our bodies need! I'm not talking about drinking coffee or soda pop or any kind of liquid that has anything added to it – I'm talking about just plain, pure water! That is the answer to all of our problems!" He drank several large gulps of water from the jug, which was now more than half empty.

"Oh, I know this is not a popular message, and the government will try to suppress it, because all the big companies, health insurance companies, pharmaceutical companies, hospitals, doctors, they all get rich because we are not drinking enough water! They won't make any money if we are not sick! They won't make any money if our bodies are healthy and functioning properly!" He drank more of the water.

"Breathing disorders, asthma, allergies, digestive system disorders, heartburn, cancer, diabetes, restless leg syndrome, insomnia, arthritis, headaches, kidney problems, high blood pressure, high cholesterol, thyroid problems, liver problems, skin problems, acne, not to mention obesity, and just about any other disease you have or can name will be cured if you just drink more water! Try it! You will be surprised! Don't take my word for it, try it for yourself!" He drank the remaining water that was left in the jug and replaced the cap.

"You might be saying to yourself, 'I don't like water.' Well, your body likes water! Your body loves water! Your body needs water! Your body craves water! I would venture to say that every single person out there watching me right now needs to drink more water!"

Kori could see the sense of what he was saying, in general, but she doubted that drinking more water could cure any disease. Besides, she had a good excuse for not drinking lots of water: at work, she could not be leaving the switcher every half hour or even every hour to go to the bathroom. It was a rare day when she could leave the control room one time during her shift, and that was usually to run to the newsroom to get clarification on spelling of a name she needed to type. She didn't have time to go to the bathroom at work. She wondered what this guy was getting out of this program, which seemed to be an infomercial.

"If everyone in the world would just drink as much water as our bodies need, as much as our bodies are craving, do you realize, that would be the beginning of world peace? Everyone would just feel so much better in their physical health, they wouldn't want to argue or fight or strive to be better than others, or even go to war!

"Some people live in areas where they can drink water straight from the tap and it tastes fine, and it doesn't smell like chlorine. But that water isn't really pure. Maybe you don't like the taste of the water in your area. Maybe the water where you live isn't really fit to drink. No problem, friends! We can keep you stocked up with a week's supply of clean, fresh, purified drinking water, delivered to your door, every week! One gallon per person, per day, at a cost you won't believe. And if you order now, we will add an extra gallon per person, per day at no additional charge!"

Kori knew there had to be a catch: the guy was selling water! She changed the channel: flip, flip, flip, looking for something to keep her awake: sports... no, watching any sport would put her right to sleep; commercial, commercial, guy movie, dinosaur movie, commercial, news, news, news; no, she had had enough news to last the rest of her life; interview program. She stopped on the interview to see if it might be about something interesting.

"If the United States and the United Kingdom and the world powers, including the United Nations, would just follow this program, we would be able to have world peace," one man was telling another man. "All wars would end."

"Are you saying that even the wars in the Middle East would cease?" the interviewer asked. "That seems impossible!"

"All they have to do, ALL of us, I should say, all WE have to do is to follow this method. These are the steps to world peace, and this is the only way we will ever achieve world peace."

"It sounds so simple, how can it work?"

"Look at these steps. They are simple. All we have to do is get the leaders of all these countries to agree to follow this 7-step process and peace is inevitable."

"We're out of time, but I just want to hold up a copy of your book again so everyone can see it," the interviewer said, displaying a book. "That book, again, is 'Seven Steps to World Peace,' by Rosh Hummhah. Get your copy now, and the announcer will tell you, if you call within the next fifteen minutes, you not only get a discount, you get Rosh Hummhah's second book, 'Three Steps Up to the Plate,' free! So call now, or you will miss out on the opportunity of a lifetime."

Kori changed the channel to a program with a woman who looked like a doctor sitting beside another woman at a desk.

"The answer is self-appreciation," the doctor lady was saying. "When we truly appreciate ourselves, then we can appreciate others. We are the highest form of being in the universe, and if we can just appreciate ourselves, we won't need to degrade others because we will be secure in who we are."

"Wait a minute, Luna," the other lady said. "You mentioned that we are the highest form of being in the universe? Are you telling me you don't believe in God?"

"You're an intelligent woman, Leslie," Luna said. "You can't be saying that you possibly believe in God, can you? I know that you are much smarter than that. You are above that level. A belief in God was necessary for the previous generations who had not yet reached their full potential. Today, we have all the knowledge and technology we need to do anything that lower-functioning brains thought a superior being would do. We have everything we need, and we have proven that a higher form of life does not exist."

"When was that proven?" Leslie asked.

"Oh, come on, Leslie, there is nothing in this universe that proves that God exists."

"Excuse me, but I beg to differ," Leslie said. "I see God in everything. He created this universe, every tree, every mountain, even you and me. Nothing could exist without God."

"Don't bring me into this silly creation-story fantasy," Luna warned. "Every intelligent person knows this world could not have been created by anyone. It came into existence billions and billions of years ago when two atoms collided."

"That theory has never been proven and it sounds about as far-fetched as the world riding on the back of an elephant standing on four turtles—" Leslie began, then she interrupted herself, "—I see we are out of time, so, thank you, Luna, for being here with us, and, to all you faithful viewers out there: until next week, stay sweet."

Kori changed the channel again: cartoons...kid shows...reruns...ah, one of her favorites, the Mary Tyler Moore show. She was so tired, she had to get some actual sleep before she went to work tomorrow; oh, no, later today. She had to be at work in less than four hours – not just at work, but alert and fully functioning. She needed to go back to sleep, even if she did return to the nightmare of murdering someone again. She just needed to close her eyes for a few minutes...

TUESDAY
CHAPTER 8

Kori blinked and looked at the clock. It was already quarter to twelve! She leaped out of bed and pulled on her clothes, grabbed her keys and she was out the door in six minutes. The ice was melting, and her car wasn't locked (she still felt uneasy about leaving it unlocked overnight, but it was still intact) so she jumped into the car, started it, and was at the station before the car heater even got warm, ready to take over for Brad by 11:55.

"Hey, Brad," she said casually, as she entered the control room.

"Did you sleep with your cat?" Brad asked.

"As a matter of fact, yes," Kori said. "I always do. Why do you ask?"

"It looks like you have a clump of cat hair in your hair," he said, "and you have a lot of interesting loops going on there."

She had forgotten to brush her hair! She smoothed it with her fingers, removing a wad of cat hair, which she placed in the garbage can. She dared not smile, because she hadn't brushed her teeth this morning. She hadn't even looked in the mirror!

"Do I have a minute to go to the ladies' room?" she asked.

"Sure, you have almost 90 seconds. Take your time," Brad assured her.

Kori dashed out of the control room and around the corner to the restroom. She filled her mouth with water and swished it around in her mouth while she combed her fingers through her hair. She spat out the water, then checked her reflection in the mirror. THAT was what she looked like today? Well, she couldn't do anything about it now; she had to get back to the control room.

"Were you up all night?" Brad asked, as soon as he ran the break and joined the network programming. He moved out of the chair so Kori could sit.

"Just about," Kori said. "After the extremely late newscast, after the baseball game ended, and after the ice storm, and after everyone else left, I finally went out to my car to find it was frozen under a thick layer of ice, about an inch thick. I couldn't get my key in the lock--"

"Whoa! You lock your car?"

"Yeah, an old habit from when I lived in the danger zone," Kori explained. "Anyway, I couldn't get in my car--"

"So you walked home?"

"No, Snorty had a blowtorch," Kori said.

"Yeah, I bet he did," Brad said.

"No, really, he thawed my lock with his blowtorch."

"That's a good one."

"No, really! But we could only get the hatchback open, so I crawled in and then I drove home."

"So, let me get this straight. Snorty used his blowtorch on your hatchback?" Brad asked teasingly. "Wait until this gets around."

"Will you just listen?"

"I'm all ears."

"You're all comments."

"Aren't you going to tell me what happened next?"

"If you stop interrupting me."

"I'm not interrupting you. What happened after Snorty put his blowtorch to your hatchback?"

"Okay, I don't like the sound of that--"

"But I bet Snorty did."

"Well, anyway, when I got home, I couldn't get out of the car because the door locks were still frozen and the hatchback only opens from the outside."

"You could have called someone to get you out."

"I don't have a phone in my car."

"Oh, that's right! The only person in the state who locks her car is also the only person in the United States who doesn't have a cell phone, not even for emergencies."

"Don't you think I thought of that?"

"So, did you have to spend the night in your car?"

"You spent the night in your car?" a male voice repeated. "Who was there with you, to keep you warm?" The same guy who had leered at her yesterday, the short, Jim Carrey lookalike, came into the control room and sat at the graphics computer, in the same seat that was her seat during the news, grinning at her in a way that made her uncomfortable.

"Kori, have you met Jim Smith?" Brad asked. "Smitty, this is Kori. She's the daytime switcher, and during the news, the AD. You be nice to her, Smitty. You hear me?"

"Hi, Kori, I've heard about you," Jim Smith said knowingly, nodding, with a lecherous grin.

"It's nice to meet you," Kori forced herself to say, thinking that he already hated her before he met her. Well, she didn't like him either. She did not see anything about him that she could possibly like.

"So, what's the story about spending the night in your car?" he asked. Kori didn't want to reveal anything about herself to this prejudice stranger.

"I didn't spend the night in my car," Kori said. "I was just telling Brad that my locks were frozen and I had to let my car run until it got warm enough inside to thaw them so I could get out." She decided not to tell them about anything that happened after she went into the building, especially about the nightmare. She just needed to be alert today, and get through the day, through the newscasts, and tonight she could go home and get a good night's sleep.

"Hey, is this your break coming up?" Jim Smith asked.

Kori panicked – she didn't have the tapes for the commercials loaded into the machine. She looked at the monitor and the log and saw that the break didn't start for another twelve minutes.

"Heh-heh-heh, just kidding," Jim Smith said.

"It wasn't really funny," Kori said.

"I made you jump, though, didn't I?" Jim Smith asked, grinning like a psychopath.

"I'll leave you two love birds here to argue it out," Brad said, as he went into the engineering room.

"So, do you have a boyfriend?" Jim Smith asked. He didn't waste any time, did he?

"No, do you?" Kori asked.

"Oh, you are so funny," he said. "Is that what it's going to be like?"

"Is that what *what* is going to be like?" Kori asked.

"We are going to be working side by side, you know," he said.

"I heard."

"So, you've heard about me?"

"No, just that you were going to be working in here."

"I'm working now," he said, leaning back in his chair. "I'm waiting for them to tell me what they want."

"I'm working, too," Kori said defensively. To prove her point, she stood up to go to the tape room to load the commercials in the tape machine.

"Don't load your tapes yet," Jim Smith told her. "We're using all the machines right now."

"I'm just getting them ready," Kori said, taking the log into the tape room. She put the tapes she needed for the breaks for the entire afternoon in order on the rack next to the tape machine. She looked at the clock, then stepped through the other door into the production room.

"Hey, Prather," she said to the main producer, "the break is in three minutes."

"Go ahead and load your tapes," Prather said. "We have to figure out these colors before we're going to need the tape machine."

"Thanks," she said, returning to the tape room. She unloaded the tapes the production crew was using and loaded the tapes for the commercial break. She set the remote, then she returned to the control room.

"What are you doing?" Jim Smith asked, panicking. "We are NOT finished with those tapes! We're going to use them RIGHT NOW!"

"Prather told me to go ahead and run the break. It starts in just a minute."

"I know, I was just messing with ya," Jim Smith said, laughing. Kori was liking him less and less every second she spent with him. How could she work every day next to a person who hated her, a person who had a mission to make her life miserable?

"Whoa!" Jim Smith yelled, pointing at the monitors. "Look at that Biff! He's a Biff! He's such a Biff? Can ya believe it? What a Biff!"

Kori ignored him.

"Oh, man, what happened to her face?" he asked. "It's all messed up! That is the kind of face I hate! It looks like her eyes were carved out of stone! I hate that kind of face! You probably like it, don't you?"

The entire afternoon, Jim Smith took every possible opportunity to bother Kori. He continuously told jokes over the headsets to the other members of the production crew, loud enough so Kori could hear. His jokes were crude and not funny. He acted like he was ignoring Kori, but she could feel him looking at her. She tried her best not to pay any attention to him, but it was hard, with his off-color remarks and the fact that he kept trying to mess up her breaks. She decided she was not going to let him ruin her day or her job. She was going to do her job, and do her best on the job, and whatever he was doing or trying to do, well, that was his problem, not her problem. The whole afternoon, the only work Jim Smith did was to type one sentence into the computer.

When it was time for them to switch places, Jim Smith stood and bowed, as if offering the chair to a queen. Kori just smiled and collected the papers she needed to begin typing the titles and captions for the news stories. It bothered her that she was sitting in the chair while it was still warm from his body heat. Jim Smith took over the switcher and, although Kori had loaded the commercials for his first break, he missed the cue and didn't roll the tape in time, resulting in five seconds of black over the air. He clumsily switched - he didn't dissolve - before rolling the tape, then he rolled the tape so the countdown showed on the air before the commercial appeared. Kori didn't say anything about it – she had had another error-free afternoon, but she didn't want to be as obnoxious to him as he had been to her, so she kept her remarks to herself. She felt like she should give him some slack; after all, it was his first day on the job.

The station manager rushed into the control room, banging the door against the wall.

"What happened?" he shouted at Kori. "I was with clients, and we saw a COUNTDOWN on the air! What are you doing, sleeping at the switcher?"

"No, I—" Kori began.

"Well, you better make sure you don't let that happen again," he said, storming out of the room. "It was completely unprofessional and uncalled for," she heard him say, as the door slammed behind him.

"I would say that was unprofessional and uncalled for," Jim Smith said.

Kori just glared at him.

"What's the matter with you?" he asked. "Why are you looking at me like that?"

Kori didn't have time to talk. She had a lot of typing to do and only a little time to finish it. When the commercial ended, Jim Smith switched to the program a few seconds late, causing him to miss a portion of the program in progress.

"Did I say something wrong?" he asked.

"You better load the next break, it's coming in just a few minutes," Kori suggested.

"Don't you think I know what I'm doing?" Jim Smith asked. "I was just going to do that right now, before you so rudely interrupted me." He got out of his chair, nearly knocking it over, and went into the tape room.

Kori inhaled deeply in an attempt to relax. She had an extremely painful headache, and her neck and shoulders were incredibly tense. She smelled an odd odor and she figured it must be a Jim Smith odor. She didn't like Jim Smith's odor, and she didn't like Jim Smith.

He returned to the control room and sat down confidently just before the break was scheduled to start. Kori noticed that the alarm light, indicating that the tape remote start was not ready, was lit. She didn't want to say anything to Jim Smith, but she didn't want to get blamed for another one of his mistakes.

"Your tape remote isn't ready," Kori told him.

"What are you talking about?" Jim Smith asked. "I just cued up that pupper myself."

"The alarm light is on," she said, pointing to the red light. She saw the cue to roll the tape, jumped out of her seat, flew through the door to the tape room and started the tape manually. "Take it!" she yelled at Jim Smith.

He switched to the commercial with only one second of black before it started.

"Not bad, huh?" he asked proudly. "I'm a professional."

Kori ignored him and returned to her typing.

"You probably won't be able to get all that typed before the news starts," he said. "That is a lot to type. There is no way you can get all that typed on time."

Kori would not be able to get it all typed if he kept talking to her, but how could she get him to stop? She didn't have even a second to tell him to leave her alone. She tried to focus on what she was doing and she tried to not hear his constant comments. When she didn't answer him, he started making comments about the people on TV.

"Whoa! Look at her! I wouldn't mind going out with her. You know what I mean?" Jim Smith remarked.

Kori didn't look up from her screen to see what the lady looked like.

"She really has a body! And a face to go with it! Man, she is a natural beauty, all over, you know what I mean?"

Kori focused on her typing.

"Wow, where did they get that car? I didn't know there were any of those left on the planet! I wonder if they had it shipped over from Russia? What do you think?"

Kori continued typing.

"Guilty! She's guilty!" Jim Smith shouted. "Don't believe her! I wouldn't trust her for a second! Would you? Look at her! Look at her! Her face says 'guilty' all over it. She's lying! She might as well be carrying a sign! Oh, man, throw the book at her!"

Kori wished he would stop talking.

"Oh, man, look at that jacket!" Jim Smith said. "That jacket is really smooth! I bet he spent a fortune on it! If I had a jacket like that, the ladies would be all over me. Of course, I mean, even more than they already are, you know. I've got to get me a jacket like that. Man, is that jacket ever smooth!"

Kori clenched her teeth as she typed quickly.

"Yep, I'm really known around here," Jim Smith said. "I'm known by the ladies, a real ladies' man, a man who really can get to the ladies. And once they get me, they never want to let me go. You know what I mean? I have quite a reputation around here. Yep, I really have quite a reputation with the ladies. I'm the man. All the guys are jealous of me. And the ladies all loooove me."

Kori couldn't say anything to Jim Smith. He just sat there with that ridiculous look on his face.

"Loser! He's such a loser! I am SO glad I'm not him! What a loser!"

He was making Kori so angry. Couldn't he be quiet for a minute?

"Ahhh, about time to roll another break," he said. "Three, two, roll it, and... take it! Beautiful! An excellent switch!" he said. Kori didn't want to look at him, but she wondered if he were breaking his arm patting himself on the back.

"Woo-woo! That's my car!" Jim Smith exclaimed. "Yep, that's my red Mustang. What a beauty! And not a scratch on it! That's my car. Oh, man, what a prize! Do you like Mustangs?"

Kori shook her head. She did not like Mustangs and she did not have any time for conversation. She typed in the weather data, statistics, and temperatures for the entire area.

"Wow, Mama!" Jim Smith shouted, then he whistled. "She is really hot! Look at her! I wouldn't mind taking the trash out with her! You know what I mean?"

Kori began typing the sports scores.

"Kitt Gormay! Look! It's Kitt Gormay! Man, I can't believe it! Can you believe it? I can't believe it! Kitt Gormay is actually on this program? I never would have guessed. Would you have ever in a million years guessed that Kitt Gormay would be on this program?"

Kori did not know how much more of this guy she could stand. Was he intentionally trying to irritate her? She tried to concentrate on her work. Until today, she had loved every moment of her job. Today, from the moment Jim Smith came into the room, she had been annoyed, angry and aggravated. This guy was really getting on her nerves. Snorty was not an ideal person to work beside her, but he was a million times better than Jim Smith.

"I love this show!" Jim Smith said. "Why don't they make shows like this any more? This is the best show ever made! This is my very favorite show of all time! Don't you just love this show?"

This was not Kori's favorite show, and now, because Jim Smith liked it, she hated it. Why couldn't he just sit there and quietly switch the show, like Barry always did? Where was Barry, anyway?

"Five minutes, everyone," Jeff announced over the intercom system. Kori put on her headset, because now was the time when last-minute changes would be made. She figured Jim Smith already knew what to do, and she hadn't been instructed to train him, so she didn't mention to him that he should put on his headset. He went into the tape room, and Barry came into the control room.

"Hey, Stranger," Barry said.

"Barry!" Kori said, relieved to see him. "Are you going to switch the news?"

"Nope, that's Smith's job tonight," Barry said, "and weeknights from now on. I'm only going to switch on the weekends."

"Oh" Kori said, disappointed.

"I just came in to be sure he has all the commercials loaded for the news. At least for awhile, I'm going to be working in the tape room during the early news." Barry left the control room to join Jim Smith in the tape room, and a moment later, Jim Smith returned to his seat at the switcher. He put on his headset.

"Smith, you there?" Jeff asked through the headset.

"I'm here, and I'm rarin' to go!" he answered.

"Barry is going to be running the commercials from the tape room," Jeff explained, "so you just need to roll the news tapes and switch the breaks. Think you can handle that, Smith?"

"I've got you covered," Jim Smith said. "Piece of cake."

"Oh, another thing, two minutes, everyone. Hey, Smith, no comments during the news, unless I ask you a question," Jeff instructed. "I'm the only one who gets to make comments, and you just pay attention."

"Yes, sir," Jim Smith said obediently. "You won't hear a word from me, not one word, unless you ask."

"Starting now. Turn off your microphone, Smith," Jeff said. "One minute, kiddos."

Kori hoped Jim Smith would get out of line and Jeff would get irritated with him, and then he would get fired, so she wouldn't have to work with him every day. Was that too much to hope?

The news started and the team worked well together, even though Kori was simmering with frustration about Jim Smith. He had such an easy job, he had great hours, he was so rude and annoying, he was right next to her all day, and he was getting the same pay as she was getting. All he had to do during the news was to switch the breaks, while she had to be concentrating every moment. She tried not to think about it so she could perform at her best – but her body was aching and she began to feel so weary, even at a time when she usually felt a huge shot of adrenaline. She felt like she needed a nap. She felt like she needed a break from Jim Smith. He had turned off his microphone, but he was constantly making comments that only she could hear. When they finally

61

finished the news, Jim Smith wanted to give Kori a high-five, as if doing their job were some great accomplishment.

"We're quite a team, aren't we?" he asked.

"Quite," Kori managed to say.

"Want to go get some dinner?" he asked.

"No, thanks, I already have other plans," she said, realizing that he was now off for the day, and she would be coming back in three hours. Now, that was a bonus; she wouldn't have to work with him when she came back after her break! She was really looking forward to her second shift. Snorty was a dream co-worker, compared to this guy.

CHAPTER 9

Kori went home – she didn't see Theo this evening - and she fixed a can of vegetable beef with barley soup and her favorite sandwich – avocado, tomato and sprouts on whole wheat bread – for dinner. Tundra jumped up on her lap and curled up for a nap while Kori was eating. When Kori finished eating, she wanted to just take a quick nap, but she didn't want to disturb Tundy. She began to pet her, and Tundra purred loudly.

"Come on, girl, let's go rest on the couch for a few minutes," Kori said. Tundra seemed upset, but she let Kori carry her to the living room. Tundra again settled on Kori's lap. Kori closed her eyes and took a deep breath, aware that she could only sleep for a couple of hours, then she needed to get back to work. All her muscles felt tense, as if she hadn't relaxed at all in days – which she hadn't. A hot bath would be very nice, she thought, as she drifted into sleep.

CHAPTER 10

Kori sat in her apartment, unable to keep her mind off her evil deed. She had escaped the scene of the murder, and not one person had seen her – well, she hadn't seen another person, anyway. Since murders never happened in this area, even if someone had seen her, they would never connect her with the crime. She didn't have any evidence on her – she examined herself and saw no blood, no signs of a struggle, no missing buttons or any personal items that could have been left as evidence at the scene.

She had gotten away with murder, and no one would ever know about it.

She knew. She would always know. She would have to keep her secret from the world forever, a horrible, condemning secret. She could never feel free again, the way she felt just yesterday... yesterday when her troubles were so far away. Now she had joined the ranks of the criminals – but they didn't know it. She was a secret criminal, a loner criminal, she had a secret life, a hidden life, a terrible secret that she could never share with any other person.

She couldn't turn herself in to the authorities – they would send her to jail forever, or sentence her to death – so she had to punish herself. She would deny herself pleasure. She would not buy anything for herself except the basics of what she needed to survive. She would get rid of her television and donate all her money to charity. She would pay for her mistake.

Why had she done it? Why had she felt as if she had had the right to kill someone? She didn't! She was wrong! She had made a huge mistake – but she couldn't admit it to anyone. She would never do it again. She would never do anything wrong again. She felt so heavy. Maybe she should just die.

CHAPTER 11

Kori was really sweating! She had had another nightmare! What was happening to her? Why did she keep having this series of nightmares? Why couldn't she change the channel in her brain? Tundra had left her lap, and Kori was sitting on the couch, covered in sweat. She looked at the clock. She had enough time to take a shower before she had to go back to work.

She had only been dreaming, but these dreams were really troubling her. As she stepped into the stream of hot water, she let her mind wander. Was she somehow connecting to someone else who had murdered someone? Was another person's mind taking over her mind when she slept? Was she mentally traveling to another person's mind? Was she seeing the future, predicting a murder, like that lady did on that movie she had seen last year? She didn't really believe things like that could happen, but she knew the human mind did have capabilities that had not yet been discovered. What was her mind trying to tell her?

She thought about her grandmother and what she would say about these nightmares. "What did you have for dinner? Those beans and that cabbage have a strange way of popping up in our dreams, while moving through our digestive systems." Kori couldn't think of anything unusual she had eaten lately.

Kori remembered a Dream Workshop she had attended in college, and one of the essays, "Can Dreams Be a Window to Our Inner Selves?" She wondered if that meant something... but why would she keep dreaming she had murdered someone?

She turned her mind to the other thing that was really bothering her: Jim Smith. He *was* a thing, an annoyance, a sub-human who needed to get some training in human relations – how to be a decent human being. How was she going to work in the same room with him, side by side, every day, with that terrible attitude he had? How could she convince one of her bosses that he needed to be moved to another position, any other position, or better yet, fired? Surely they had to notice that he was not necessary, and really, he was a hindrance to the production crew. Maybe she should say something to Jeff or Prather. Somebody had to do something about the situation! Jim Smith could not be allowed to continue as he had begun.

She got out of the shower feeling a little bit better about everything, but still, she was very tired. She tried to feel energetic due to the fact that she didn't have to work with Jim Smith when she went back to the station this evening, but that didn't really compensate for all the sleep she had missed the past couple of days. Today was only Tuesday, and she was scheduled to fill in for another switcher on Saturday, so she had a long week ahead. Well, tonight after the news, she would come home and go to sleep. She would play some relaxing music on her stereo and NOT dream that she had committed a murder.

As she walked down the hallway from her apartment, she felt as if she were growing taller with each step she took. The ceiling seemed to be closing down on her as she became a giant! She looked behind her, at apartment door, just down the hall, and then ahead of her, down the hallway. Now she was shrinking, getting smaller with every step! The ceiling was getting higher and higher! She reached the door just in time to open it and return to her normal size. She really needed to get some sleep! She hoped to be renewed by the fresh air, but it didn't help.

"Hey, are you going to work?" Theo called from his balcony, as Kori was walking to the parking lot.

"Yes!" she said. She didn't feel like talking to him, even though he was not nearly as annoying as Jim Smith.

"Say hi to all the famous people for me!" Theo yelled.

Kori smiled. He was kind of funny. She had to give him a break; after all, he was just trying to be friendly. He was not trying to get under her skin, like Jim Smith was. Theo was just being a nice neighbor. Maybe she should be a little bit nicer to him – as long as it didn't lead to anything more, like spending time with him.

"Hey, Julie Moore's brother!" Theo shouted.

"I am NOT Julie Moore's brother," a man replied.

"Well, I'm telling you, you look EXACTLY like Julie Moore!"

As Kori got into her car, the name 'Moore' popped into her head. Julie Moore, Mandy Moore, Mary Tyler Moore: why were all these Moore names in her life right now? What did it mean? She shook her head. It meant she was really tired, and things were starting to not make sense so much that they were making too much sense, they were making Moore sense.

"Moore," she said aloud, as she drove to the TV station. "Moore. Mooooore. Moooo! Moooo! Moooo!" She laughed. Yes, she was very tired.

"So how do you like Jim Smith?" Snorty asked, the moment Kori stepped into the control room.

"I don't," Kori said.

"I knew you would hate him, because he hates you."

"I didn't say I hate him, I just said I don't really like him."

"You hate him, I can tell."

"I didn't say that."

"You don't have to say that, I can tell. You hate him."

"I don't hate him. You don't know what's going on inside of my head," Kori said, thinking, thankfully, no one knows.

"I know what's going on inside your heart," Snorty said, "and you hate Jim Smith."

"He's annoying, okay? And right now, so are you."

Snorty just laughed and rolled the break as Kori sat down and began to type the evening news titles, scores and weather graphics. The evening passed quickly and Kori was ready to leave as soon as the news ended. She just had a few things to finish before she could go home.

"So are you looking forward to another day with Jim Smith?" Snorty asked.

"No, I am not!" Kori said. "Just drop it, okay? I don't want to talk about Jim Smith any more."

"I knew it, you hate him."

"I don't hate him. I just don't want him to be the subject of my conversation."

"You hate him."

"I don't hate anyone, but right now, I am close to hating you," Kori warned.

"You can't hate me," Snorty said. "You love me."

"Oh, please," Kori said. "You wish!"

"No, I don't! I told you, you're not my type."

"That's right, everyone loves *you,* but you are in love with Rose."

"Shhh! Don't let anyone hear you say that!"

67

"I knew it! You like her!" Kori said. "Okay, I've got you! Every time you mention Jim Smith, I'm going to mention Rose."

"Okay, you win," Snorty said. "But I know you hate him."

"And I know you love her!"

"Stop saying that!"

"Okay, I'm out of here," Kori said. "You got everything under control?"

"Sure do," Snorty assured her.

Kori drove home and went straight to bed. Tundra snuggled up on top of Kori's head and they both fell asleep.

CHAPTER 12

Kori sat in a room full of people, knowing she was guilty, hoping the other people wouldn't discover her guilt. They arranged the chairs so they were all in a semi-circle around her chair. They sat facing her. Everyone looked at her expectantly. She didn't want to see their faces, the faces of the ones who were condemning her, but she noticed a man in an overcoat with greasy, stringy hair and a woman in a white dress who looked like Betty White. Kori looked at the floor and saw a pair of fancy, shiny red shoes beside a shiny red purse, and she wondered whose feet were in those shoes, but she didn't want to make eye contact with anybody. She was on center stage but she could not perform. She had no idea what to do or say.

She had murdered someone. She had killed someone. They all knew she was guilty of something, but they didn't know exactly what she had done. As long as she did not confess her crime, they would not know how terrible she was. They might be able to excuse her, if they didn't know she was the worst kind of criminal: a murderer. Her mind would never be free, but she dared not reveal her horrible secret to anyone. Nobody would ever be able to forgive her, knowing that she was a most terrible person, that she had committed the worst crime.

She would be an outcast from society. She could do that to herself, but she couldn't let someone else do that to her. She would go away and live in solitude, out in nature, not bothering anyone and not causing any more problems. She would be able to get away from everyone – but she could never escape her conscience.

Where was her boyfriend, anyway? Why wasn't he coming to her rescue? Wait a minute, what did he look like? Who was her boyfriend? She really loved him, she depended on him, but where was he? Who was he? How could she ever explain to him what she had done? She would have to break up with him. She would rather break up with him than share with him the burden of her awful secret.

CHAPTER 13

Kori opened her eyes, disoriented. Who was her boyfriend? Where was she? Oh, yes, she was in this apartment, and she was NOT guilty of murder. She hadn't had a boyfriend in a long time, not in years, not since she left the Pacific Northwest, not since she and Paul Pardo had parted years ago.

She let the memory of Paul Pardo creep into her mind again. She had loved him. Her heart pounded now as she remembered him. Paul was so handsome, so smart, so kind; he had been everything she could ever want in a man... he was just a boy, actually, when they met in grade school. Kori had always liked him – he was the first boy who ever kissed her, when they were just in the fifth grade, and he was about to go on vacation with his family for the summer. He begged her for just one kiss, to seal their commitment to each other, one secret kiss under the big cherry tree in the privacy of her back yard. They promised each other they wouldn't tell anyone about the kiss, and for the next few years, Kori couldn't look at Paul without her face turning red. They had very few classes together, so they didn't see each other often, but she always kept him in her heart, as her special one, and she compared everyone else to him. None of the other boys were as cute or as smart or as clever as he was. When they reached high school, they naturally came together as a couple, studying together, going to football games and dances together, and planning to spend their lives together.

Kori smiled at the thought of Paul Pardo. They had gone to different colleges, Kori in Seattle and Paul in Boston, but they had pledged to be together as soon as they graduated. They had spent their Christmas and summer breaks together, finding it more and more difficult to be apart from each other. Kori had been on the verge of quitting school when she went to visit Paul in Boston for Christmas of their junior year, but Paul urged her to stay in college until she graduated. She had longed for him to propose to her, to give her an engagement ring to seal their commitment to each other; she would not have stayed with him in his apartment if she hadn't expected them to eventually get married.

Their nights spent together had been wonderful, almost magical. On the morning she was to catch her flight back to Seattle, Kori had suggested that she stay in Boston and get a job. She couldn't stand for her time with Paul to come to an end.

"You have to go back and get your degree," Paul told her, gathering her things.

"I just want to stay here with you," she protested.

"You know I won't be able to concentrate if you stay here. And you have to finish school. Be patient. I am. We have the rest of our lives to spend together, after we graduate."

"I don't want to wait."

"We have to wait. The time will pass quickly – we're more than halfway finished with college."

"I could transfer here," she said. "Then we could be together now."

"We need to do everything in the proper order," Paul insisted. "Besides, if you stay here and get pregnant, you will ruin everything for us. That would destroy our entire lives. We don't have room in our lives for a child right now. Let's not get ahead of ourselves. First, we both finish college, then we can make plans for what will happen after that."

"I don't care if I finish college," Kori cried. "I want to be here, with you, now."

"You are being selfish," Paul said. "You are not looking at the big picture of things."

"Why don't you want me here?" *He* wasn't looking at the big picture – wasn't their plan to get married?

"I want to stick with our plan, and that plan does not include you staying here now."

"All I want is to be with you," she cried.

"You have to go, right now," Paul insisted. "Look, if it is so hard for you to leave, maybe we should just cool it and not see each other until we graduate. It won't be hard to part if we are not together."

"What are you saying?"

"You just go home, and this coming summer we will both work, and save our money for the time we can be together."

"I want us to be together now."

"We can't be together now!" Paul shouted. "I'm beginning to think it was a mistake for you to come here for Christmas."

"A mistake?" Kori asked, hurt. "The time we spent together was a mistake?"

Kori had gotten on the plane and, a few weeks later, she had learned what a mistake their time together really had been.

WEDNESDAY
CHAPTER 14

"Hey, Kori-Kori-Bo-Bori!" Jim Smith called, as soon as she entered the control room the next day at work. She had decided she was going to be nice to him, to give him another chance.

"Good morning," she said.

"Kori-Bori. Hey, your name rhymes with 'boring,' you know that?"

"It does not."

"Yes, it does! Kori-Boring!"

"That's not a rhyme."

"Yes, it is!"

"No, it's not." Why was she arguing with him over something so trivial?

"Yeah, it is. Wow, what did you do to yourself? You look much older than when we first met," he said.

"We just met yesterday!"

"I know! Isn't that weird? Look at you! Wow!"

All afternoon at work, Jim Smith was even more obnoxious than he had been the previous day, constantly making rude and crude comments, bragging about himself, and criticizing and belittling Kori. Kori was extremely sleepy – she had only had a few hours of sleep in the last two – or was it three? – nights, so she was more irritable than usual. She couldn't ignore Jim Smith – he was so loud, and he was always in her way. Three times he nearly messed up her breaks by turning off the remote to the tape machine at the last minute, after Kori had set it. Once, he tripped her – an accident, he said, then he mentioned that she was rather clumsy. Kori couldn't stand Jim Smith. He was unable to be nice to her.

"Let's have a stare-down," he suggested.

"No, thanks."

"You just know you can't win."

"I don't want to have a stare-down."

"You're just staring at the monitors."

"I'm watching them! That's my job!"

"You know you would lose."

73

"I don't want to have a stare-down."

"Chicken."

"I don't want to have a stare-down." She couldn't imagine staring at him.

"Loser."

"I'm working!"

"So am I."

"I don't want to play games while I'm working."

"Your loss, not mine. I know I would win."

"Don't you have something to do?"

"I'm doing it."

"Can you work without talking to me?"

"Oh, you think you can work without talking to me? Fat chance, Loser."

Although she was provoked, she bit her lip and didn't respond. He made a big huffing sound and turned to the computer, mumbling about how she was a chicken-loser and she was just afraid of competing with a winner.

During the news, Jim Smith kept making vulgar comments that only Kori could hear. He seemed to be nice and respectful to everyone else, but he constantly needled Kori.

She was so relieved to get through the newscast and go home for dinner.

CHAPTER 15

As Kori approached her apartment building, she saw Theo on his balcony. She couldn't avoid him - he was looking right at her.

"Hi Kori!" he shouted as she walked up the sidewalk.

"Hi," she said with a sigh.

"You really look tired," he said. "Are they making you work too late at the TV station?"

"No, I'm fine," she said, irritated.

"You don't look like you are fine," he said.

"Leave me alone!" Kori shouted. "I am perfectly fine!" She fumbled in her purse for her keys. Her purse fell from her hands, and she knelt to collect her belongings that had spilled on the sidewalk.

"I'm sorry, Kori, I didn't mean to say anything wrong," Theo said.

"No, I'm sorry, I didn't mean to snap at you," Kori said. "You're fine, and you've been really nice to me. It's just that I haven't had much sleep lately, so I guess I'm a little cranky."

"Are they working you too hard at the TV station?" Theo asked excitedly. "Do you have to spend too much time with all the celebrities?"

"No, it's not that," Kori said. "Really, it's not important. I just need to get some sleep."

"Why? What's the matter, Kori?" he asked, truly concerned.

"Really, it's not important." To admit out loud that her nightmares were keeping her awake seemed ridiculous in the light of day, in the light of reality.

"If there's anything I can do, just let me know."

"Thank you, I appreciate it," Kori said, "but really, like I said, it's not important."

"If it's a – you know – umm, female kind of problem, you should ask Mother Florence for advice," Theo said.

"Mother Florence? Who's that?"

"You don't know Mother Florence?" Theo asked, surprised. "I thought everyone in the building knew Mother Florence. She knows just about everything about just about everything, and she's really nice. You're going to just love her. She is so nice. She's like a mother to everyone. That's why everyone calls her Mother Florence. Want to meet her? I can take you over to meet her right now."

"No, thanks, I appreciate it, but really, I'll be fine. After my shift tonight I'll be able to get some sleep," Kori said, trying to convince herself that she would indeed be able to sleep tonight. "I need to eat dinner and then get back to work."

"Hey, do you want to come in and have dinner with me?" Theo asked. "I made my specialty: spaghetti with meat balls, with my own famous secret sauce."

"Thank you, but not tonight," Kori said, feeling guilty that she had snapped at Theo for no reason. She finally found her keys.

"Rain check!" Theo called, as Kori entered the building.

She was so tired, everything was bothering her. She wasn't feeling hungry at all – she was just tired. She didn't want to lie across the bed, because she might not be able to awaken for her next shift; and she was afraid of having the nightmare, which seemed more real every time she returned to that place of condemnation and guilt.

A shower, a long, hot shower was what she needed. Tundra joined her in the bathroom and as soon as the hot water began to relax Kori, Tundra began to yowl.

"It's okay, Tundy-baby, I'm just taking a shower," Kori said.

"Yeeeeoooowwwl."

"Good girl, just relax, I'm okay."

"Yeeeeooooooowwwl."

"Tundra, stop that."

"Maow-reep! Maaooow-reep!"

"Tundra! Be quiet!"

"Yeeeeeooooooowww!" Tundra howled. "Yeeeeeooooooowww!"

"Quiet, girl!"

"Yeeeeeooooooowww!"

"Tundra, be quiet!"

"Yeeeeeooooooowww!"

Kori could not take a relaxing shower until she found out what Tundra needed, so she quickly finished her shower, with Tundra yowling the entire time. Even Tundra was irritating Kori. She needed some sleep!

She went to the living room and sat on the couch, not wanting to turn on the television. Tundra jumped up onto her lap. Kori took a deep breath, and she seemed to be watching a movie on her wall as she stroked Tundra's silky fur. She watched a clown and a beautiful woman as they pulled discarded food from a huge garbage bin, excited to find a package of ice cream that had not yet melted.

Kori shook her head to clear the images. Was she having waking dreams? She thought she remembered something from school, a teacher saying that if the body – or no, if the brain – is deprived of going through a stage of dreaming for a certain amount of time, the person would begin to dream while he was awake. She dismissed that theory in her case – she had been dreaming, she just didn't like her dreams enough to stay asleep. Her body was lacking sleep, her mind was not lacking dreams.

She pulled herself together to get ready to go to work. Something didn't feel right in her head. She looked at a magazine on the coffee table and it was oddly unfamiliar. How did a person read? She began to panic. These are words on a page, she thought, each shape is a letter... what do they mean? She forgot how to read! Her brain was chug-chug-chugging instead of flowing, and she couldn't think! Words, what were words?

She sat on the couch and closed her eyes. She needed to recharge, reconcile, remember! She couldn't let herself fall asleep. What should she be thinking? Food... dinner... maybe she needed to eat. She wasn't hungry at all – nothing sounded appetizing – so she looked at the floor to see if it could give her any ideas. She stared at the patterns on her carpet, needing to memorize them, as the lines and squares moved back and forth. She had to remember those patterns!

Kori gently moved Tundra off her lap, onto the couch, then quickly stood and did several jumping jacks. She felt a little dizzy, but she had to move her sluggish body. She decided to go back to work, even though she would be nearly an hour early for her shift. She couldn't do anything here at home right now. She put on her coat and grabbed her keys. She bumped her shin on the coffee table, then she bumped her head on the door as she was opening it. She recalled her mother mentioning – years ago – that when a person is tired, he is more likely to have an accident than when he is fully rested.

"Mom, you are right again," Kori said aloud. "I just proved it." She tripped on a bump on the carpet in the hallway and she almost fell. As she turned the corner to go down the steps, the pocket of her coat caught on the end of the handrail, pulling her back with a jerk, nearly causing her to tumble down the steps. Her heart beat wildly as she steadied herself. She would have to be extra alert while she was driving to and from the TV station tonight.

Kori thought about her mother and father. She hadn't seen them in more than two years. She had been so busy with work, volunteering to work on holidays so her coworkers whose families lived in the area could stay home on those days. She loved her parents, but they were a world away from her, going on with their lives, while she was establishing her career. For just a moment, she wished her parents lived closer to her; then she remembered that she was happy and satisfied with her independent lifestyle. Living near her family could be beneficial in some ways; however, her life was going in a different direction. She needed her freedom and personal space. Her parents had loved Paul and they couldn't understand why she had ended their relationship.

CHAPTER 16

Kori arrived at the TV station and went into the control room.

"Go for the big one!" Snorty was shouting at the TV when Kori arrived.

"Hey, Snorty," Kori said.

"What are you doing here?" Snorty asked.

"I work here."

"I know that."

"So, why do you ask?"

"Just wondering what you're doing here."

"I work here."

"He-he... hey, how are you and Jimmy Smith getting along?"

"We're not."

"I would love to see you together," Snorty teased.

"We're not together."

"You guys sit side by side, all afternoon, every day."

"We're not together."

"He's been here two days. So you've been together two days," he chuckled.

"We are NOT together!"

"You don't love him?"

"No! No WAY!"

"You hate him, don't you? I knew you would."

"Just stop!" Kori said, then she remembered her defense. "So, have you seen Rose tonight?"

Snorty giggled.

"Is that a yes?"

"She dropped off some tapes," he said, embarrassed.

"Did you talk to her?"

"Who?" he asked, stifling a laugh.

"You know who I mean," Kori said. "Rose, your new love."

"Shhh! She is NOT!"

"Sounds like true love to me," Kori said, as if she were an expert on true love.

"So, what are you doing here, anyway?"

"Um, it's my job. Like, I work here, you know?"

"Why are you so early tonight?"

"No reason, I'm just here," Kori said. "I'm going to get an early start, so I won't have so much last-minute pressure." She sat in her chair at the graphics computer and looked through her run-down sheets. She only had a few titles to type. She had arrived way too early. As she looked at the computer screen, the colors seemed to shift and exchange places. She found herself staring at the colors, watching the letters grow and shrink before her eyes. She felt so comfortable sitting there, with no pressure on her. The words began to glow on the screen as she watched them. She could just keep staring at this screen all night.

"Kori! Wake up!" Snorty's voice brought her back to the station. "What's the matter? You tired or somethin' or what?"

"No! I mean, yeah, kinda."

"You been staying up too late, thinking about Jimmy Smith?"

"Oh, come on!"

"What is it? You got insomnia?"

"No, I wish I *could* sleep."

"What are you talking about? You don't have insomnia, but you wish you could sleep? Why can't you sleep?"

"I just have... I just haven't been able to sleep," she said, unable to tell him the real reason.

"Hey, did you see that last commercial? You could take some of those pills. They'd put you right to sleep."

"No, I hate taking pills," she said. She hadn't thought about pills. She wondered if taking sleeping pills might stop the dreams. She immediately dismissed the idea. She shook her head. "No pills."

"Hey, maybe you could be in that study at the University, you know, the one where people are trying to find out why they can't sleep."

"I already know why I can't sleep," she said.

"Oh, you do? Why?"

"It's not that important."

"You can't sleep, and it's not important?"

She couldn't tell Snorty that she hadn't been able to sleep lately because she was having nightmares that she had murdered someone. Here, it seemed so ridiculous, not logical; besides, she didn't want him to try to analyze her dreams, or to try to figure out what was going on inside her head.

"Man, I need to get to work here! Quit bugging me!" Kori said.

"Oh, I get it!" Snorty said, "You've got a boyfriend!"

"No way! That's not it! That is definitely NOT it!"

"Who is it?"

"No one!"

"It's Jim Smith, isn't it?"

"No way! No WAY!"

"Ah, no wonder you don't hate him! Oh, I get it! Hate is just another side of love! What was that song about that?"

"You're crazy! Do you have a grain of a brain in your head? I don't have a boyfriend, and if I did, it would never in a million years be Jim Smith!"

"I know, I know," Snorty teased. "That's what they all say."

"Hey, better be quiet, here comes Rose," Kori warned.

Snorty's face turned red as Rose came into the control room.

"Here are the graphics for the governor story," Rose said, handing a paper to Kori.

"Thanks," Kori said, "I'm right on it."

"Right on," Rose said. "Hey, did you see my new car?"

"You got a new car?" Kori asked, amused at how Snorty inconspicuously came to attention. "What kind?"

"A Chrysler Sebring convertible," Rose answered.

"That white convertible is yours?" Snorty asked, clearly impressed.

"That white convertible is mine," Rose said, smiling.

"It's a real beauty," Snorty remarked.

"Oh, sorry, I didn't notice it," Kori said.

"I'll take you for a ride sometime," Rose promised. Snorty looked as if he hoped to be invited also.

"Okay!" Kori said. "I'm looking forward to that! I'm sure it will be quite a ride!"

"Oh, it's smooth," Rose said, turning to leave the control room. "You're going to love it."

Snorty smiled as if he were floating on a cloud. "So, you're going for a ride with Rose," he said.

"Yep. We're going for a ride," Kori said. As she typed in the titles for the newscast, she kept making typing mistakes. Her fingers just didn't do what she wanted them to do. Her mind felt awake, but her body seemed to be disconnected and dull. She kept her eyes on the screen, watching as if someone else were typing the words. At the end of a word, she saw the final letter repeat across the screen, indicating that her fingers were resting on the keys. She blinked her eyes and shook her head in attempt to clear it, to get her head and body back in sync with each other. She had to get herself together to be ready to do the news. When Snorty left the room to load the tapes, she stood up and did twenty-five jumping jacks to get her blood flowing. She could do this; she was feeling great and completely alert now.

Ken came into the control room – a rare thing for him to do, since he normally didn't come in contact with the lowly production workers – and put a tape on the table for the news without saying a word. Ken watched the wall of monitors as if they were the living things in the room, then he exited with his head held high and proud. Kori doubted that he had even noticed she was in the room; he had just been in a room full of machinery.

"Kind of brings a chill into the room, doesn't he?" Snorty asked as he entered the control room with an exaggerated shiver.

"He's like a robot," Kori remarked, shaking off the uncomfortable feeling Ken had left in the room. She wondered if he had any feelings. She took a deep breath. She was ready for anything.

The news finally began and she made it through the entire newscast without making any mistakes. She hurried back to her apartment. She needed sleep; deep, uninterrupted sleep. She felt her stomach growl with hunger as she drifted off to sleep, consciously reminding herself that she needed to remember to eat in the morning.

CHAPTER 17

Kori hurried across the street, hiding under the cover of night, which was so dark, she almost couldn't see which way to go. She didn't know the exact route to follow to get out of this part of town, but she knew which direction she needed to go away from the tall brick building with the dead body in it. As she rounded the corner, she literally bumped into a police officer and fell to the ground.

"You all right, Miss?" he asked, extending his hand to help her to her feet. His hand felt hot on her cold fingers. He smelled of cigars and bad breath.

Kori tried to speak but her mouth was full of gum and her words sounded like a jumble of mumbling. She stood to her feet and pulled the gum out of her mouth. Some of the gum was stuck to her teeth. She pulled and pulled, like a magician pulling trick handkerchiefs out of his mouth, with gum coming out of her mouth, and more gum coming out of her mouth, but more and more gum still there.

"You all alone out here tonight?" the officer asked.

Kori kept pulling gum out of her mouth. She tried to answer, but the gum was still stuck to her teeth and she couldn't get all of it. She had to get rid of the wad of gum before she could say anything, or be coherent.

"You shouldn't be here," the officer said. "You are in the wrong place at the wrong time."

Still, Kori couldn't speak, pulling more gum from her mouth. It stretched and stretched. She kept pulling it.

"You just can't get away unless you explain yourself," he warned.

"I-moffflleebuum," Kori said, still pulling gum, stretching it out of her mouth. She just couldn't get it off her teeth! It was stuck between her molars!

"Where have you been tonight? What have you been doing? Where are you going?"

"Home," she managed to say, scooping out more gum.

"And do you have an alibi?" he asked. "Maybe we need to go down to the station and get to the bottom of this."

"Fo- wha-?" she said, wishing she could just get all of this gum out of her mouth so she could speak freely.

"You are acting mighty guilty, I have to say. Why don't you tell me all about it?"

"Nothing," she mumbled over the wad of gum still in her mouth.

"Did you do it? Or are you trying to say you are innocent? I think we need to go down to the station. You have no reasonable reason to be here. You need to come with me, young lady. You are acting very suspicious, and you are not going to get away with it. You can't get away with anything. You can't hide from the law. You can't hide from yourself. You know what you have done and what is inside has to come out. You are guilty, and you know it."

Kori shook her head but she knew her guilt was written all over her face. She was unable to speak.

"You are going to be locked up for a long, long time, unless you confess and come clean right now. Are you going to tell me, or not? Or are you going to put yourself in jail for life? What is more important to you? What are you going to do? Do you enjoy being a prisoner?"

Kori awakened in a pool of sweat. Why did she feel so guilty? She had not committed a crime! She WAS free! She was not in prison!

The room was still dark. Kori blinked her eyes to focus on the clock: it wasn't even midnight yet! She needed to go back to sleep and get some rest, but these nightmares would not permit her to get the rest she needed. Her eyelids were so heavy, she couldn't stay awake any longer – she had to return to her alternate existence as a guilty murderer.

She wanted to run away from the scene of the murder. Her feet were so heavy – where were her rollerblades? Oh, no, she couldn't skate in the dark, but she needed to move quickly and she couldn't. The end of the block was so far away from her, and the more steps she took, the farther away from her the corner was. Maybe she should get off the sidewalk and try to run on the street. How would being in the street help if she couldn't lift her feet? She could remove her shoes; where were her shoes? She looked at her bare feet and hoped she had not left her shoes – or any physical evidence – at the scene of the crime. Where had she left her shoes?

Where was her purse? Had she left it in the apartment with the dead person? She thought about the old cliché, 'a criminal always returns to the scene of the crime.' She would not return to the scene, and that would mean she was not the murderer, not in anyone else's eyes, anyway.

She knew she was guilty, though, and all of her running would not get her away from the burden of guilt she had to carry for the rest of her life; but she couldn't stop and get caught. Oh, what a relief it would be if she could just stop and rest – no, she couldn't even think about it, she had to keep dragging her heavy legs, one after the other, and get away from here, far away, as fast as possible.

CHAPTER 18

Kori tried to move her legs. They wouldn't move! She realized they were tangled in her covers. She was at home, in bed. She was not trying to run away from the scene of a murder. Her legs were aching and tired from all that running: wait, she hadn't been running, so why were her legs so very tired? Why was her heart pounding? She was not guilty of murder. She was not guilty of a crime. She was a good person, asleep in bed in her room, in her own home, having another nightmare, in the middle of a dark, dark night.

Perhaps her room was too warm, and that was why she kept having such bad dreams. She opened the window and inhaled the fresh air. Now, she should be able to get the horrible images – the horrible feelings – of the dream out of her head. She thought about beautiful things: a sunset, a colorful bird, flowers, the baby Maureen was soon to deliver, and when would she have a baby, or when would she meet the person she would marry, to be the father of her future children? Who could ever live up to the high standards set by Paul Pardo? She had yet to meet a man who was as nice, as kind, as loving, and as handsome as Paul; and even if she met a man who had most of those good qualities, what were the chances that he would be interested in her? She was not a bad person, but she wasn't a beauty, the kind of woman to attract men. She was a smart person when it came to figuring out problems and puzzles, but she knew her social skills were lacking. She was shy around most people, and really, she was a loner. She didn't want to end up like Snorty. He was 40 years old, he had never had a girlfriend, and he was just waiting to meet the right woman who would want to love him and take care of him in his old age.

She refocused on beautiful things: flowers, nature, lakes, the ocean. She did not want to be thinking about her future – or her lack of a future – in the middle of the night when she should be sleeping. She wanted to think of good things and go to sleep and have a good dream. Even sleeping without a dream would be a nice idea. Maybe she could get some sleeping pill and take just one, so she could get a good night's sleep. Sleep, sleep, sleep, it was a funny word: sleep. Who had ever come up with that word? She started to giggle, and she disturbed Tundra, who looked at her with an annoyed expression on her face. Wait, why could she see Tundra so well in the dark of her room? She looked at the clock and saw that it was nearly seven in the morning. She had been sleeping, but she was not rested. She could go to sleep for a few more hours before she had to go to work, and she was going to sleep, determined to have good dreams or no dreams, good dreams or no dreams; dreams, dreams, dreams, another funny word. Who invented this language, anyway, with all these funny words? It must have been someone with a great sense of humor who wanted people to laugh at the funny sound of words.

"Words, words, words," she said aloud. That was the funniest sounding word of all! "Woooorrrrds. Weirds. Weirdo. Wordo. Waldo. Waldorf."

Suddenly she felt tears spring to her eyes. She was really lonely. She was alone with her cat, unable to sleep, saying funny words that made no sense. She was pathetic. Her career was on a plateau the size of a mesa in the Grand Canyon, she had no meaningful relationships, she was far away from her family, she had money in the bank and no desire to spend it. She had lost her appetite for life. She didn't matter to anyone. Jim Smith had gotten the good job, and he hated her for no reason. He was such a jerk – even jerks hated her. She was lower than a jerk!

What was her purpose in life? Was her entire life's purpose to add graphics to the news? Or was it to stick commercials in television programs so people could watch broadcast TV? How many people were even watching their station these days? They didn't want to watch broadcast stations that had to abide by broadcast standards. People wanted to watch cable stations, where the actors were free to cuss and swear and display private body parts for all to see. Kori was becoming insignificant, soon to be obsolete. If she were to disappear, would it make any difference in the world, or here, in this town, or at her job, or in this apartment building? People would miss Theo if he were gone, because he was so friendly. He was able to reach out to people. Kori wasn't like that. She always waited for someone to reach out to her – and that was the problem right now. Nobody was reaching out to her, no one was reaching for her, and she was sinking. Even if she could reach out, to whom would she reach? She couldn't think of a single person... her parents... a co-worker... Paul Pardo? No, he had advanced far beyond her level. She wasn't good enough for him anymore.

Maybe that was her problem – she wanted someone who was way out of her class. Maybe she was on par with Jim Smith, but she still wanted Paul Pardo to reach for her. Maybe she wasn't even up to the level of Jim Smith; maybe she was even beneath him. Where did she belong? Where should she be? Did this world have a place for her? Did this world have a man for her, so she could share her life with someone, her hopes and dreams?

Oh, no, she couldn't share her dreams with anyone. She didn't want to ever share those horrible nightmares with any other person... or maybe she should share them. She could write them and make them into a book, or a scary movie about someone who couldn't get away from nightmares of murder. No, what a dumb idea; who would want to experience those nightmares, again and again? She couldn't stand it! Why would she want to share such an awful experience with anyone else?

THURSDAY
CHAPTER 19

She couldn't go back to sleep. She needed to start her day, make some breakfast, clean her apartment, keep her mind occupied. She got dressed and went into the kitchen, greeted by an awful odor coming from the garbage can. She would start by taking out the trash. She pulled the plastic bag out of the garbage pail and took it downstairs to the trash bin behind the apartment complex. As she reached to open the door to go back into the building, the door swung open and hit her on the head, knocking her to the ground.

"Oh, Kori! I'm so sorry!" Theo said, coming outside with a bag of trash in his hand. "Are you alright?" He tossed his bag into the bin and bent down to examine Kori.

"Um, yeah, everything seems to be in working order," she said, as he helped her to her feet.

"Oh, you have a bump on your forehead," he said. "Are you crying? Your eyes are really red. I'm so sorry!"

"No, I just put in my contacts," she lied. Why couldn't she just tell the truth? Why couldn't a person ever tell someone, 'Yes, I was crying?'

"Here, come in and sit down," Theo said, guiding her into the hallway. Kori let him lead her.

"My apartment is right here," he said. "Don't worry, you'll be fine. I'll call Mother Florence to come over."

"What for?" Kori asked. She was fine now.

"You have received a bump on the head," he explained, opening his apartment door.

"Did I hear you call my name?" an elderly lady asked, coming out of a nearby apartment.

"Mother Florence!" Theo said. "This is Kori, the one I was telling you about, the famous lady who works at the TV station."

"Kori, it's nice to meet you," Mother Florence said. She had gray curls, a soft voice, and very kind blue eyes.

"Kori just got a big bump on her head," Theo said, before Kori could respond. "It was my fault – I hit her with the door.

Accidentally! It was an accident! Really, I'm so sorry. Here, sit on this chair."

"It's nothing, really," Kori said.

"Look at that bump!" Theo said.

"Do you have any ice?" Mother Florence asked.

"I don't need any ice on it," Kori said, shuddering at the thought of ice on her forehead. She was freezing.

"I was going to bring over some lemonade, but my ice maker isn't working," Mother Florence said.

"Oh, I'm sorry," Kori said.

"Don't be sorry, you didn't break it," Theo said.

"No, I mean – I don't know what I mean," Kori said.

"Ow, that bump must be taking effect on your brain," Theo said.

"No, it's just, I was just trying to, I was just saying, I mean..." Kori wasn't sure what she meant.

"The lemonade can wait," Mother Florence said. "You need to just sit quietly for awhile. That's quite a nasty bump on your head."

"Really, I'm okay," Kori insisted. "Is it bleeding?"

"Nope, no blood," Theo said, examining her bump closely.

"Sometimes we need to just sit and quietly wait on the Lord," Mother Florence said gently. Kori hoped she wouldn't be getting a religious lecture, but Mother Florence was being very kind. Kori obediently sat quietly.

"Maybe we need to call Dr. Bones McCracken," Theo said. "Dr. Bones McCracken, we have a patient who needs you!"

"Dr. Bones McCracken?" Kori asked. "Who's that?"

"You don't know who Dr. Bones McCracken is?" Theo asked, amazed.

"Should I?" Kori asked, wondering what she had missed.

"Shhh, shhh, don't worry about it," Mother Florence said.

"Obviously you never listened to the Ace Trucking Company," Theo said. "If you did, you would know who Dr. Bones McCracken was."

"Ace who?" Kori asked.

"Shhh, quiet," Mother Florence said. "You don't need to trouble your mind over some silly stuff."

"They were silly," Theo said.

"Who?" Kori asked.

"Ace Trucking Company."

"Theo, just let Kori rest and don't try to fill her mind with silly stuff," Mother Florence said. "Keep your mind stayed on the Lord and He will give you perfect peace. That's a promise."

Kori had no idea what she meant. She turned to Theo. "So, is Theo short for Theodore?"

"No way!" Theo shouted. "I am NOT a Theodore! I am NOT the middle chipmunk! Really! No WAY! I'm not a Theodore!"

"Then what is it short for?" Kori asked, amused that he was so upset to be thought of as a Theodore.

"It's short for Theophilus," Theo said.

"Theophilus?" Kori asked. "I haven't heard that name before."

"It's a biblical name," Mother Florence said. "It means one who loves God, or friend of God."

"I do love God," Theo said. "Don't you?" he asked Kori.

"Um, yeah, sure," she said. She hadn't given it much thought. "I guess."

"Either you love Him or you don't," Mother Florence said. "You can't just kind of love Him, or guess that you love Him. The real question is, do you love His Son, Jesus?"

"I don't know," Kori said. "I don't really know."

"He loves you," Mother Florence said, as if He were right there in the room with them. "He died for your sins."

"I don't have any sins. I'm a good person," Kori said, in a attempt to convince herself as well as Mother Florence and Theo.

"I'm sure you are," Mother Florence began.

Theo's phone rang, but he made no move to answer it. His answering machine took the call.

"Hi-hi-hi, good friend!" the machine said. "Theo here, well, actually, I'm not here, or if I am here, I am not able to speak to you at this very moment, so please leave a message so I know you called and I can call you back. If this is a medical emergency, hang up and dial 9-1-1. Have the most wonderful day!" Beep!

"Theo, where are you? This is Bobby. Isn't this your day to be here now? See ya!" Click.

"Oh, man, I'm late for work!" Theo said, rushing around the apartment, gathering things.

"Where do you work?" Kori asked.

"I have my own business," he said. "I shovel snow in the winter and mow lawns whenever there isn't snow. I have a schedule, and today I need to be at the Henderson's, I should be there right now, because they're having a wedding at their house tomorrow and they need everything done on time, in order. I'm not usually under such pressure like this."

Kori smiled at his perception of pressure.

"Plus, I'm a writer," Theo added.

"Really? What do you write?" Kori asked.

"Well, I want to write a novel, but I have a long way to go."

"Have you written anything I might have read?"

"Well, there is one thing lots of people have read," Theo said, "but it's not really that important."

"Tell her what you wrote," Mother Florence said, obviously proud of his accomplishment.

"Well, okay, here goes," he said, clearing his throat. "Here goes! 'Hand dryers protect the environment. They cut down on trees being cut down to be turned into paper towels. They warm your wet hands. They are more efficient to use than paper towels, because they save trees. Dry with warmth and joy.' So, what do you think? Have you read it?"

"At least a hundred times," Kori said, smiling. She figured since someone had written it, why couldn't it have been Theo?

"I've got to get going. You can just stay here and rest," he said to Kori. "Mother Florence will take good care of you."

"No, thank you, I can go home now," Kori said, wondering where she put her keys. She stood to her feet. Her head was throbbing, but she didn't know if it was due to the bump on her forehead or because she was still so tired. Mom was right, accidents do happen when a person is tired.

"Do you want me to walk you to your door?" Theo asked.

"No, you need to get to work," Kori said. "I'll be fine."

"I can walk with you," Mother Florence offered.

"No, thank you very much, but I can make it," Kori insisted. She walked slowly to the door, then she stopped. "I appreciate everything you did. Thank you both so much." She felt a lump begin to catch in her throat. They had been so kind to her, and they didn't really even know her.

"Come on over any time," Theo said, as Kori entered the hallway.

"And you'll have to have a rain check on that lemonade," Mother Florence insisted.

"Thank you," Kori whispered, unable to stay any longer. They were very nice to her. They had shown her kindness she didn't deserve. As she opened the door to her apartment – she hadn't taken her keys because she hadn't locked the door – her mind made a connection to something she had been thinking earlier today. She had a hard time reaching out to people – as a matter of fact, she didn't know how to do it at all – but today two strangers had reached out to her. She didn't consider Theo and Mother Florence to be her friends, but she did begin to consider them. Tears flowed down her face.

CHAPTER 20

Kori arrived at work feeling cranky, irritated, and not at all rested. Jim Smith was sitting in his chair in his usual position: leaning back with his hands folded behind his head. He was making comments into the headset when he noticed Kori coming into the control room. Brad smiled at Kori and headed toward the engineering room, nodding at Jim Smith behind his back.

"He's all yours," Brad said, leaving the room.

"Thanks," Kori mouthed, making a face at Brad.

"So, what's your favorite song of all time?" Jim Smith asked Kori.

"I don't know," she said, looking at the log, not wanting to have a conversation with him. "I don't have one."

"Oh, come on," he said. "You MUST have a favorite song of all time."

"Well, I don't," she said, trying to find anything else to do instead of talking to Jim Smith.

"What song do you like?" he asked.

"I like a lot of songs," she said, sighing. She was just too tired to deal with Jim Smith today.

"What song springs to your mind right now?" he asked.

"I don't have a song springing in my mind right now."

"A little grumpy, are we, today?"

"Are we?"

"Come on, just name a song."

"The only one I can think of right now is 'Don't Stand So Close to Me.'"

"Oh, you like The Police?" he asked. "I love them! I love The Police! They are SOOO good! They are the best! They are my favorite band of all time!" He completely missed Kori's intended hint.

"I can't stand them," she said.

"Oh, man, Sting, oh, he has the best voice! I just love him! Don't you just love his voice? He's so great! You know what I mean?" Jim Smith was a little too enthusiastic about this.

"I can't stand his voice," she said, trying to pay attention to the soap opera on the monitor.

94

"Are you kidding? He's the greatest! I mean, the very greatest!"

"I don't think so."

"What about Air Supply?" he asked. "Aren't they great? They are so good! 'I'm all out of love...'" he screeched.

"I can't stand them either," Kori said. "Why do you like the groups with the wimpiest vocals?"

"What do you mean? Who has a better voice than Sting?"

"What about the greatest voice of all time, Freddie Mercury?"

"Who's that?"

"The lead singer of Queen. He was, anyway. You have heard of Queen?"

"Queen? You mean Queens of the Stone Age?"

"No! Queen! 'We Will Rock You,' 'You're My Best Friend,' 'Bohemian Rhapsody.' 'Another One Bites the Dust.'"

"Nope, doesn't ring a bell."

"'Play the Game.' Liar.'"

"I am not a liar! I'm telling the truth!"

"Not you, it's one of their songs. You must have heard 'We Are the Champions,' 'Killer Queen,' 'Don't Stop Me Now,' You know, Queen."

"Queen? Can't say I've ever heard of them."

Was he kidding or being serious? "You haven't heard of Queen? How old are you, anyway?"

"Dare you ask my age?" he asked, acting very upset. He wasn't a good actor.

"No, I don't really care, I just can't believe you've never heard of Queen. They have all those songs on commercials, you know, 'I Want to Break Free,' 'Driven by You,' 'Under Pressure.' You've heard them."

"I never watch commercials," he said.

"What are you talking about? You work in a TV station, in the production department, producing commercials all day long! You have to watch commercials! It's your job!"

"I don't pay any attention to them. And when I go home, I turn on my big screen TV and I watch movies, not commercial television."

"You never watch regular TV?"

"Never. I get enough of that here."

"You haven't even been here a week."

"I know, and I already had my fill of commercials."

Kori didn't know why she was arguing with Jim Smith. She didn't have the energy for this. She needed to pay attention to the TV program so she could be ready to run the break, and save her energy for news time.

Why did all the guys have a big screen TV? Well, she didn't care. She just wanted to get through her shift and not think about those awful vocalists Jim Smith liked.

"Makin' luuhhh--uuuv… out of nothin' at all," Jim Smith sang, off key and out of tune.

"Please don't sing," Kori said.

"You like it, don't you?" he asked.

"No, I don't,"

"Sure you do."

"Don't sing in this room, please."

"When I really get moved by one of my favorite groups, I have to sing."

"If you get moved, can you just move out of this room to sing?"

"Can't do that."

"Just don't sing."

"I'm not going to make any promises."

"You don't have to make any promises, just don't sing."

"I love to sing, don't you?"

"I don't love to sing, and I don't love it when you sing."

"You don't mean that."

"I mean it."

"No, you don't."

"Yes, I do."

"You do love it when I sing."

"No, I don't."

"You don't mean that."

"Yes, I do."

"See? You do love it. I told ya!"

Kori went into the tape room to be sure the tapes were loaded for the break. Jim Smith was really getting on her last nerve. Didn't he have any work to do? She glanced into the production room and saw that it was empty. She looked on the studio monitor and saw the rest of the production team in the studio having a conference with the clients, so Jim Smith really didn't have any work to do until they finished their meeting and decided what they wanted for graphics. How could she get through the afternoon with him talking to her all day? She would have to just ignore him and pay attention to the soaps.

She returned to the control room and rolled her break. As soon as the commercials were over and Kori joined the network again, Jim Smith started talking.

"I love that guy, don't you?" he asked, referring to the sleaziest character on this program. "He always dresses so sharp, and he always gets the best girls."

He always cons the best girls, Kori thought, but she didn't want to jump into another conversation with Jim Smith, so she didn't say anything.

"I wonder what kind of cologne he wears?" Jim Smith asked. "Maybe I could get some. I'm sure that scent would definitely attract the ladies."

"Look, this room is too small for all kinds of smells, so please, don't wear cologne to work," Kori begged.

"It would be nice. You would really love it."

"I don't wear perfume to overwhelm all you guys in here," Kori said.

"Maybe you should," Jim Smith said. "Like Rose, she always smells so good."

"Oh, not you, too?"

"Me too? Who else thinks she smells good?"

"Oh, never mind," Kori said, not wanting to give away Snorty's secret.

"Who? Who is it? Come on, you can tell me. Who likes Rose? Come on! Tell me! I won't tell anyone! Is she dating someone? Who is it? Who does she like?"

"Everyone!" Kori said. "Everyone thinks she smells good, and she does. I love her rose perfume."

"You are jealous, aren't you?" Jim Smith asked. "You are jealous because she is so beautiful and sexy, and you, well..."

"What? What about me?"

"Never mind. You're just not like Rose. She's beautiful and sexy."

He implied that Kori was not beautiful and not sexy. She decided to just drop it – after all, he hated her. He could say anything just to bug her. Unfortunately, it was working. He was bugging her.

"I'm going to start working out," he said. "Yep, I'm going to be so buff, all the ladies will just fall all over me." He looked to Kori for a response. When she didn't say anything, he continued. "Yep, I'm going to go to the gym every day and turn this into a six-pack that you won't be able to resist. No woman will be able to resist me, I'll be so buff. I'm going to buff up and I'll be huge. Yessiree, when I start working out, the ladies will follow me where ever I go. I'll be buff and I'll have to get a body guard, so I can just select the ones who are really fine, and keep the dogs away."

"Are you referring to women as dogs?' Kori asked, angered.

"No, I'm just calling the dogs 'dogs,' you know what I mean?"

"No, I don't know," she said, then she wished she hadn't spoken to him. Why was she letting him bother her?

"I'll be so buff, women will be calling me twenty-four/seven. Yep, I'm going to be so buff—"

"Will you stop saying 'buff'? Don't you have work to do?"

"I am working! That's the beauty of it! What's wrong with being buff?"

"Nothing, you are just over-using the word, okay? You have reached the quota for the day, as a matter of fact, for the week. I wouldn't mind if you never say that word again in my presence."

"Oh, you love it, and you know it. Buff! Buff! BUFF!"

"You have no idea what I love and what I don't love! But I don't love that word!"

"You are so hostile today. Did you get up on the wrong side of the bed?"

She didn't want to talk to him any more, but he just wouldn't leave her alone. She didn't answer his question.

"Oh, kind of touchy, are we? Are we having problems at home? Maybe problems with your boyfriend? Who is your boyfriend, anyway? Do I know him?"

He was trying to irritate her, and she didn't want to give him the satisfaction of knowing that he was succeeding.

"Come on, you can tell me. I'm a good listener. Is he trying to get you to do something you don't want to do?"

No, but you are, she thought, you are trying to make me talk to you and I don't want to talk to you.

"Do you guys live together? Because I just heard that North Dakota is the only state in the United States where it is illegal for a man and woman to live together if they are not married. You could be arrested, you know. It's the law! You better watch out."

"What are you talking about? I don't have a boyfriend right now."

"Oh, you're in between guys, huh?" Jim Smith snickered. "I like the sound of that, you know what I mean?"

"Will you stop?"

"You don't want me to stop, you know what I mean?" Jim Smith teased. "You like it and you know it."

Kori decided to not answer him any more. Didn't he have any work to do? Or was his job just to torture her? He wasn't doing anything else today.

"Do you think I'm buff enough?" he asked, after one blessed moment of silence. "Maybe I don't need to work out, you know what I mean? I already drive the ladies crazy. They are all over me. I can't have just one, because all the others will get jealous, you know what I mean? I tell them, I go, 'you fine ladies will just have to share me.' There's enough to go around. No shortage on what the ladies want from me, nosirree. They want it, I got it, and it's all theirs, and I mean, all they want, you know what I mean?"

Was he really expecting an answer from her, or did he think she already knew what he meant? Every time he said the phrase 'you know what I mean,' Kori felt an alarm going off in her head, like a fire alarm, screaming. She didn't want to know what he meant, she didn't care what he meant! She couldn't understand anything he was saying except, 'you know what I mean.'

Jim Smith began to ramble. "Abbabaabaaabbbaaaabbaa, you know what I mean? I could really dadadadadadadaaaddaaa, you know what I mean? You should see me when dididididididididididididid, you know what I mean? If I win the lottery, I'm going to rudrudrudurudurudurudu, you know what I mean? I wouldn't change my lifestyle at all, I would just tuptuptuptutptuptpuuptup, you know what I mean?" People are always saying it, but I really mean it, you know what I mean?"

"That's great," Kori said, just to stop the flow of unnecessary words from his mouth.

"You really think so?" he asked. "Or are you just saying that? Do you really mean it? I mean, sometimes people just say that, you know what I mean? But you wouldn't do that, would you? Or would you? You know what I mean?"

Kori had no idea what he meant; she just wanted him to be quiet. Why couldn't she just tell him the truth, that she wanted him to stop talking to her? His voice was really annoying her, like fingernails scraping across a chalkboard. It was as if the very tone of his voice was grating inside her spine, each word drilling into her core. She just couldn't stand him. She was glad he hated her, but did he have to actively hate her? Couldn't he just passively hate her, by ignoring her? That was the way she wanted to hate him, by just ignoring him; but how could she ignore a pest that would not leave her alone?

What could she use as a pest repellant against him? Could she point him toward another target? She noticed Brad through the window in the engineering room, checked to see when her next break was starting, then she went to the engineering room.

"Brad, he won't stop talking," she said desperately.

"Just do what I did," Brad said.

"What's that?"

"I told him, 'Smitty, you're an idiot, and I don't listen to idiots,' and then he began to show me some respect and now he leaves me alone. He won't talk to me unless I talk to him first – and I only talk to him if it's an emergency. We've had one emergency this week, and he's left me alone the rest of the time."

"I can't call him an idiot," Kori said. "That is not politically correct."

"I'm just telling the truth, and he knows it."

"I can't use that word," Kori said.

"Why, do you have too much respect for him? Don't tell me you like him? Come on, Kori, I think I know you better than that."

"No, I just don't call people names."

"Well, it's your funeral," Brad said.

Kori cringed. That phrase really bothered her.

"Want me to tell him to get off your back? Hey, Smith!" Brad said.

"No, that's okay! I'll deal with him," Kori said, although she had no idea how she would do that. She returned to the control room to run the break.

"Bradsville is pretty cool, isn't he?" Jim Smith asked, obviously having watched their conversation through the window.

"Bradsville?"

"Yeah, he likes it when I call him that, you know what I mean?"

"Oh, yeah," Kori said. How much more irritating could Jim Smith be?

"What's your favorite team of all time?" he asked her.

"I don't have one," Kori said, hoping he would dismiss the conversation.

"Who do you like better, the Lakers or the Jets?"

"I like both."

"But which one is better?"

"Are you serious?"

"Yeah, who do you think will win?"

"Win what?"

"The playoffs, what do you think?"

He was from 'Dumber and Dumbest,' that's what she thought.

"They won't be playing each other, I can tell you that," she said.

"Sure they will! West Coast meets East Coast, you know what I mean?"

"Do you have any idea what you are saying?"

"Of course I know! I have all the cable sports packages. I'm a sports buff, the ultimate sports fan!"

"Sure you are."

"I am! I'm all into sports!"

"Do you know that the Lakers are basketball and the Jets are football?"

Jim Smith looked at her blankly. "I think the Lakers are going to win the playoffs," he finally responded, nodding. He had such a ridiculous look on his face.

He turned his chair to face her. Her mind seemed to go numb. She could see his mouth moving so she knew he was talking to her, but all she could hear was the sound of a train roaring, as it came from the distance and invisibly passed right in front of her, between them. When the train was gone and the sound subsided, Jim Smith's voice came into focus and she began to understand that he was saying words. Even when she could understand his words, she couldn't make any sense of what he was saying. He turned away from her, to his computer monitor.

Now Kori had an extremely bad headache. She stared at the wall of monitors and heard Jim Smith's voice in the background as an annoying buzz-buzz-buzz, with an occasional 'you know what I mean?' followed by a brief pause. She was very tired and suddenly hungry. Had she eaten breakfast today? She couldn't remember. She would need to go to the store after her shift, during her break. Her forehead was throbbing... did she have an accident earlier today? What had happened to her head? She felt kind of dizzy. The screens in front of her face began to blur and then they merged together, overlapping, as she stared at the moving lips of one of the actors, hearing the buzz-buzz-buzz of a pest in the room. Her head was so very heavy... patches of dark blue and black began to fill in her field of vision until she couldn't see anything, bzzz...bzzz...bzzz...

"Kori? Can you hear me?"

Kori heard a voice from far away, way down a tunnel. She knew how to move her lips, this was English she was hearing, a person talking... how could she respond?

"Bzzzz-mmmmm."

"Maybe we should call 9-1-1," she heard somebody say.

"I'm all right," Kori's voice said, from a distant corner of the room, without her controlling it.

"Are you sure?" That was Brad's voice, but she couldn't see him. She saw patches of black and blue.

"What happened?" Did she ask that question, or was she being asked that question? She didn't know.

"Zubb-zubb-zubb-zubb," someone said.

"Kori, are you with me?" Brad asked.

As Kori came out of her haze, she heard a voice but she couldn't make any sense of it. She couldn't see anything but a dark gray background, and each word she heard made a square in her vision, adding squares across until the row was filled, then the next row began filling. It was as if she were staring point blank at the detail of the fabric of long underwear, each square of fibers filling with each word she heard. The voice was a buzz-buzz-buzz, each buzz adding a square to the pattern.

Kori blinked and shook her head. What was happening to her? Was she having some kind of seizure? A large hammer in her head began pounding, pounding, replacing the buzzing with a huge thump she could feel shaking her entire body as the pain pulsated from her head down her spine.

"What happened?" another voice asked, a familiar voice, a nice voice... Maureen's voice.

"Shehoodahoodahoodahooda, you know what I mean?" Kori heard.

"Did she faint?" Maureen asked.

"I think so," Brad's voice answered.

"Maybe she's pregnant," Jim Smith said.

"James B. Smith!" Maureen said sharply. "In the first place, just because a woman faints, it doesn't mean she's pregnant, and secondly, pregnant women hardly ever faint!"

"It's a fact that—" Jim Smith began.

"You need to get your facts straight," Maureen said. "Kori, come with me. Brad, can you cover for her for a few minutes?"

"Sure, as long as Smitty doesn't make ME faint," he said.

"What? What did I do?" Jim Smith asked. "I didn't do anything, you know what I mean?"

As Kori's vision returned, Maureen led her to the newsroom lounge where reporters sometimes rested when they worked double shifts or stayed to do the news during weather emergencies. Only the members of the news team had a key to this room. Maureen helped Kori get settled on a couch, then she sat beside her in a big rocking chair.

"Do you know what happened, Kori?" Maureen asked.

"I'm not sure," Kori answered.

"You have a big lump on your forehead."

"I think I got that this morning at home."

"Are you okay?"

"Yeah, I think so."

"You look really tired."

"I am. I haven't been sleeping well."

"Are you worried about something?"

"Not really, it's just..." Kori paused. She had to just say it, no matter how silly it sounded. "I have been having a lot of nightmares lately, and they are keeping me awake."

"Nightmares? You haven't been able to sleep because you've been having nightmares?" Maureen asked.

Kori felt foolish. She nodded, embarrassed.

"I have really been having some doozies," Maureen said.

"You?" Kori asked.

"Yeah, I don't know if it's because of the baby, or what, but I keep dreaming that I lose the baby," she said. "Not that I lose it, as in having a miscarriage, I keep dreaming that I have the baby, then I can't find it. I don't even know if it's a boy or girl, but after it's born, either it gets smaller and smaller until I can't see it, or I just put it down somewhere and then I can't find it."

"That's weird," Kori said.

"So, what are your nightmares about?" Maureen asked, as if this were sharing time.

"I don't – I really – I just–" Kori didn't want to tell her about her nightmares.

"Well, if you want, I can give you the name of a good psychiatrist, a woman, and she will give you the first session free. If you don't like her, you don't have to go back. I have her card on my desk. Remember that story we did last month? Doctor Killingsworth, that was her name. She's really nice. She's in the business because she really wants to help people."

"Dr. Killingsworth?" Kori asked. Her name was quite appropriate, considering the content of Kori's nightmares, but Kori wasn't sure this was at all what she needed. "Do I need to see a psychiatrist?"

"Maybe if you go see her once, you can just get some relief and then you can sleep. She comes highly recommended."

"By people with nightmares?"

"Yeah, and with all kinds of problems. Look, it can't hurt. It's free. You need to be able to get some sleep."

Maureen was making sense. Maybe Dr. Killingsworth could help her, and then she could get back to her normal sleeping pattern and her normal life.

"Do you want me to call her for you?" Maureen asked.

"No, thanks," Kori said. "That would be kind of weird, like you thought I was crazy or something."

"No! I didn't mean that! I just mean, because I know her. Oh, everything you tell her will be confidential. I just thought you might want me to set up the first appointment or talk to her and tell her you're my friend."

Maureen thought of her as a friend! Kori was surprised to hear that.

"I really appreciate that, but I can call her," Kori said, now convinced that going to see a psychiatrist would help her get some sleep again.

"You can use my name as a reference," Maureen said, then she began to laugh. "I mean, one crazy person referring another; no, just kidding, you know! I'll go get her number for you."

Kori felt relieved, more than she had in days. She was going to get some sleep!

CHAPTER 21

Kori drove to the grocery store on her way home. She needed to get some good food. She could get some broccoli and cauliflower; she felt comforted when she thought about tree-shaped foods. She was glad the store wasn't too far from her apartment, it was just around the corner... where? Where was the store?

She didn't know where she was! She was disoriented. Where was she going? What was this place? Was she awake, or was she dreaming again? Where was the store? Which way was she going?

She pulled the car to the side of the road and shook her head in an attempt to regain her bearings. She looked around the neighborhood and she couldn't see anything familiar. She slapped her arm – ow! That hurt! She was not dreaming. She made a u-turn and drove several blocks before she saw the grocery store. She had driven right past it without even seeing it! As she sat at a red light, a car began to honk. It honked and honked as she stared at the red light. She couldn't go until the light turned green – oh, oops, she was looking at the stop light at the next corner, one block ahead! Her light was green. She drove to the store and pulled into the parking lot. As she parked the car, she took a deep breath. What had happened to her impeccable attention to detail?

Kori got out of the car and she felt herself automatically walk into the store, as if she were just going along for a ride in her own body. She didn't have a list, and her brain just wasn't thinking of the food she needed. She tried to force it to think: what were the staples, what did she have, what did she need, what did she like? She could get some eggs, and chicken sounded good. What should she get first, the chicken or the egg? She began giggling. She had known her body needed rest; now she knew her brain needed rest. She was judging grapefruits when she saw her brother across the produce section! What was he doing here?

"Matthew!" she called. "Matthew!"

He didn't turn toward her or even stop when he heard his name. Kori rushed over to him and prepared to smother him with an enormous hug. Just as she approached him, he gave her the strangest look.

"Matthew! What are you doing here?" she asked, thrilled to see him.

"Do I know you?" he asked. He was always teasing her.

"You big joker!" she shouted.

"Seriously, I'm not Matthew," he said solemnly, and his face transformed into that of a stranger. Kori blinked. He had curly hair like Matthew's and he was tall and thin like Matthew; however, he was not Matthew, after all.

"Oh, I'm so sorry," Kori said.

"No, don't be sorry, I'm glad I'm not Matthew," the man said. "I am perfectly satisfied being just who I am."

"I thought – I mean - um - you look just like my brother," she said.

"Is he good-looking?" he asked.

"Oh, yes, he's very handsome," Kori answered.

"Well, thank you. I'll take that as a compliment," he said, as he continued gazing at the vegetables on display.

Kori found the cauliflower and broccoli, paid for her purchases and went home to fix dinner.

CHAPTER 22

That evening at work, after making an appointment with Dr. Killingsworth, Kori felt so much better than she had felt all week, just knowing she would be getting some relief. She had an appointment for the next morning, before she started her shift. Fortunately, someone had cancelled an appointment, leaving an opening for Kori, and she was confident that this psychiatrist would be able to help her. She would be able to sleep again!

She was typing titles into the computer and Snorty was staring at the wall of monitors when Rose entered the control room. Before Kori could say anything, Rose winked at her and smiled.

"Hey, Snorty," Rose said, "I heard about how you helped Kori the other night with her car situation. Do you think you can help me?"

Snorty whipped his head around to face Rose.

"Sure, Rosie," he answered eagerly. "What do you need? Don't tell me you're having a problem with your new car already?"

"The car is fine, but I locked my keys inside. Can you help me get them?"

"Aren't you a native around here? Why did you lock your car?"

"Oh, you know, a brand new car, I thought I should."

"You and Kori are two of a kind. You are the only people I know who lock their cars."

"So, can you help me?"

"Don't you have a spare key?"

"Yeah, at home in my apartment."

"You should keep a spare key in your purse."

"I know, and from now on, I will, I promise."

"Well, I have a Slim Jim in my truck."

"Slim Jim? That sounds pretty sexy," Rose said.

"How is a pepperoni stick going to help you open a locked car?" Kori asked.

Snorty giggled. "Not that kind of Slim Jim. This is a tool to open cars without the key, like policemen use."

"That sounds illegal. Why do you have one?" Rose asked.

"So I can help ladies in trouble, like you."

"Really? How often do you use it?"

"Never. You're my first."

"I'm honored!"

"Well, let's go," Snorty said, excited. "Kori, can you watch the board for me for a minute?"

"Sure, go ahead," she said, smiling, wondering how long it would take him to catch on to the joke.

"This shouldn't take long," Snorty said, beaming with confidence.

"Not long at all," Kori said under her breath.

They had been gone from the control room for about thirty seconds when they came back, laughing.

"Oh, you really got me," Snorty said to Rose. Rose was laughing hysterically.

"How'd your Slim Jim work?" Kori asked, smiling.

"She really got me," Snorty said, with a huge grin on his beet red face.

"Didn't you notice when you came to work that the top was down?" Kori asked.

"I wondered how long it would take you to catch on," Rose said, still laughing.

"I know! I saw it this evening when I got here, and I completely forgot!" Snorty said, laughing with them.

"So, Kori, are we still on for Saturday?" Rose asked.

"Saturday? What's Saturday?" she asked.

"We're going for a drive in my new car," Rose said.

"Oh, yeah! Don't you have to work Saturday?"

"Evening shift, not during the day."

"Me too," Kori said. "Where do you want to go?"

"I don't know. It doesn't matter. Let's just drive around."

"Sure! Wherever you want to go is fine with me," Kori said. Snorty seemed to be ignoring them while he faced the wall of monitors, but Kori thought his ear was turned to their conversation, the same way a cat's ear would turn to listen.

"Oh, Rose!" Kori said.

"Yeah?"

"Uhhhh…" Kori said, "oh, I forget. Wow, I lost it, just that quick."

"You'll remember, if it was important."

"It was SO important, for a second."

"Well, let me know if you remember," Rose said.

"I will. You'll be the first to know." Kori had no idea what she had been about to tell Rose. She searched her mind, but it was gone, as if it had never been there."

"So, did you catch up on your sleep last night?" Snorty asked, after Rose left.

"Not really," Kori said. "But I'm taking care of it."

"What do you mean?"

"Nothing, I'm just taking care of it," Kori said. She didn't feel like explaining everything to Snorty, or to anyone else, except, maybe, the psychiatrist.

"Taking sleeping pills, huh?"

"No! NO way!" Kori said loudly.

"The way you answered me didn't really sound like you are telling the truth," Snorty said.

"It IS the truth."

"Say 'cabbage.' "

"What?"

"Say 'cabbage.' "

"Why would I say that?"

"Say 'cabbage' three times."

"I don't think so."

"Come on, just say 'cabbage,' and I'll know if you are telling the truth."

"What are you talking about?"

"It's a 19th century lie detector."

"You lost me a long time ago, like, in the 19th century."

"If you can say 'cabbage' three times without laughing, you're telling the truth. If you can't say it three times without laughing, it means you're not telling the truth."

"Did you make that up?"

"No, it was passed down from my great-great-great-great grandmother, generation to generation."

"That is one of the weirdest things I've ever heard," Kori said.

"It's not weird!" Snorty said.

"It IS weird."

"Well, maybe it is weird, but it works. Try it. Then I'll know if you are telling the truth or not."

"I'm telling the truth, just believe me," Kori said. "Am I always going to have to prove to you that I'm telling the truth? Who do you think I am, anyway, Jim Smith?"

"What do mean by that?"

"Nothing."

"No, really, what do you mean?"

"He just talks too much, that's all."

"It just seems like it because you hate him."

"I don't hate him. He just bothers me."

"That's because he hates you."

"I have work to do," Kori said, turning her attention to the computer. She finished typing all the titles except the weather, and Rob wouldn't bring them until he had the last-minute temperatures after the news started. Kori started to giggle.

"What's so funny?" Snorty asked.

Kori giggled harder. She couldn't tell him she was laughing just thinking of saying 'cabbage.' He was right! If she didn't tell the truth, 'cabbage' made her laugh. She wouldn't give him the satisfaction of knowing that.

FRIDAY
CHAPTER 23

Kori nervously walked up the sidewalk to Dr. Killingsworth's office. The sign with her name on it told Kori she had the correct address, but the building was just a big, old house.

Suddenly she heard the sound of about 50 people laughing and she looked to see where they were; no, not a laughing sound, a squawking; no, a clucking; no, a barking sound; no, what was it? She didn't see anything that could give her a clue - then she looked up to the sky and saw the source. A huge flock of Canadian geese was flying right over her head, honking, honking, honking loudly. How many were there? Two, four, five, ten, fourteen, twenty, twenty-three... why was she compelled to count them? Did it really matter how many geese were returning to Canada? Remember what Dad had often said? 'Never look up when birds are flying overhead.' She quickly lowered her head and looked straight at the house as she approached the steps. She needed to get some sleep!

Last night she had had three more nightmares that she had murdered someone. The last one had been so realistic, when she had awakened, she had a hard time deciding whether or not she had really killed someone. Of course, she hadn't – she was not guilty. Her horrible, torturing dreams were just getting in the way of her reality, stealing her sleep and her sanity.

She stood on the porch and watched the geese until they were out of sight – although she could still hear them honking. She changed her mind – she didn't want to be here. She didn't want to talk about her dreams or about her life to this doctor, a stranger. Snorty had given her a better suggestion – she could go buy some sleeping pills.

A man opened the front door from the inside and almost hit her with it when he came out of Dr. Killingsworth's office-house.

"Watch out," he said, scampering by her, not looking directly at her, but focusing his gaze on the ground.

"You must be Kori," a woman said. Kori was trapped. She couldn't leave now. "Come on in." When Kori hesitated, she asked, "You are Kori, aren't you? I'm Dr. Killingsworth."

Kori was taken aback by the doctor's appearance. She was short and round, with curly, orange hair that looked like fringe on her spherical head. Her little round head sat on her rotund body, reminding Kori of a snowman with the center snowball missing; no, in her rust colored attire, she looked more like a tiny pumpkin sitting on a giant pumpkin. Kori felt herself blushing, and she hoped her face wasn't turning orange.

"Come on in," Dr. Killingsworth repeated.

Reluctantly, Kori followed her into the house, which had an odd odor, like some kind of incense or something, and everything had a sort of a green tint. The walls in the front room were lined, ceiling to floor, with bookshelves full of books. Kori followed the doctor to a barren room with wood paneling and several easy chairs. Dr. Killingsworth flopped down into one of the chairs, causing the entire house to shake.

"Have a seat," she said to Kori.

"No couch?" Kori asked. She thought everyone who went to a psychiatrist was expected to lie on a couch.

"No, I don't want you to go to sleep," she said. "I do want you to be comfortable, but not that comfortable."

"I am tired, but I don't want to sleep," Kori said, wanting to get this finished as soon as possible.

"I have a questionnaire for you to complete, but you can do that when we finish talking," the doctor said. "I can't reach it now, it's over there, on the desk." Her arms flapped by her sides uselessly.

Kori didn't respond. She wondered how could this doctor, who didn't seem to be able to take care of herself, help others? Kori was not at all comfortable.

"Why are you here?" the doctor asked.

How could Kori answer that question? Wasn't that a question for a pastor or scientist, or at least for her parents, who had brought her to life? Or was she asking why did Kori live here? She couldn't answer that one either: the roads of life had just led her here, to this job, to this city.

"What can I do for you?" the doctor asked.

"Oh, yeah, well, I just--" Kori began, not knowing what to tell her.

"Yesterday when you called me, you sounded desperate," Dr. Killingsworth said. "So, are you going to tell me about it?"

113

Now Kori felt pressured. Why couldn't she lie on a couch and stare at the ceiling, instead of looking at this pumpkin pie-faced doctor? She glanced around the room and saw a certificate on the wall. Somehow, this comforted her, seeing that the doctor had credentials. She had gone to school. She had earned a degree. Maybe she had just gotten a little off-track, or maybe she had an eating disorder, or maybe she had a thyroid condition; certainly she was qualified to listen and diagnose a simple problem with nightmares. After all, dreams weren't even real, so why should they have any power or influence over waking life? Kori was ready to talk now.

"Would you like something to eat or drink?" Dr. Killingsworth asked, after several moments of silence.

"No!" Kori answered; she had almost had her first statement formulated in her head. "I mean, no, thank you, not right now, I'm fine. In the sense of not being hungry or thirsty, I mean, I'm not really fine, or I wouldn't be here, would I? I mean, I'm fine, I'm not crazy or anything, but I'm satisfied right now, I mean, physically, I mean, I'm not – I mean, thank you, but, no, thanks."

"Why don't you just start by telling me a bit about yourself? Don't worry about the time. The first session is complimentary, even if you talk for an hour. I want to get to know a little about you."

"I live alone with my cat, um … my family lives in Washington state, that's where I grew up. I have one brother, back in Washington, and I work with Maureen at the TV station, you know her."

"Are you a reporter?"

"No, I work on the production team. I work on the news, but in the control room."

"Fascinating! I have always wanted to do that!"

Kori didn't know how to respond to that – and the doctor had broken her train of thought.

"What else?"

"Well, let's see… I'm not married—"

"Divorced?"

"No, I've never been married."

"Lucky."

"No, it didn't have anything to do with luck. It was my choice."

"Are you a lesbian?"

"No! I mean, no; I mean, no, I'm not. I'm just single, and I haven't met the right man yet."

"You haven't? Are you sure?"

"Yes, I'm sure. I would know him if I met him."

"Do you know many single men?" Why was she asking?

"Yeah, I work with lots of them, but none of them are my type. I haven't had a boyfriend since I was in college."

"Tell me about him."

"We broke up during our junior year - too many miles between us. He was really nice, but we just couldn't be together."

"I know what you mean."

Did she know? How could she know? Kori continued, "Anyway, the reason I'm here is because lately I've been having nightmares, really bad ones, and I can't sleep. I don't want to return to that world."

"What do you mean? Do you have science fiction nightmares? Are they like Stephen King or Ray Bradbury? Maybe you could write a book about this other world of your dreams."

"No, I didn't mean it like that. I keep having a dream, or a series of dreams, that I killed someone, and it's really bothering me. I don't want to live in that reality."

"Why is it bothering you?"

"Wouldn't it bother you if you kept dreaming you had killed someone, and you had to keep suffering feelings of guilt? I mean, I feel so guilty, like my burden will never be lifted."

"Who did you kill?"

"I don't know. I never see the person. I'm always just trying to get away from the dead body."

"Was it someone you know?"

"I don't know, I never see him, or her."

"Do you have any family here?"

"No, they all live on the West Coast, Pacific Northwest area."

"Do you feel guilty that you live so far away from your family?"

"Not really. I came here to establish my career, and I really love my job."

"Are you afraid of taking responsibility for your life?"

"No, I've been doing that for years now, I mean, living on my own."

"That's a song."

"What?"

"That's a song, 'Living on My Own' you know?"

"Oh, yeah, I think I've heard of it. Anyway, back to my nightmares..."

"Dreams are most often representations of something in our lives, either in our current life or our past, or our fears, or just in our own minds. Dreams are not usually literal, they are representations."

"Okay," Kori said. What good was that explanation?

"You sound like you are having a classic nightmare about killing someone. Do you hate your boss?"

"No, I like him."

"Is he married?"

"Yes."

"Do you hate his wife?"

"No, she's really nice."

"Are you jealous of her?"

"No, I don't want to kill her."

"Not physically, but representationally, perhaps?"

Was the doctor inventing words?

"No, I like her," Kori insisted.

"Are you jealous of your brother?"

"No."

"He is the one your parents love more. He is closer to them, and he is reaping all the benefits, while you are a distance away from them and unable to connect with them."

"No, I love my brother. I don't want to kill him."

"It's not that you want to kill him; you think you already did."

"No, I don't think that."

"It sounds to me like a classic case of regretting that your childhood is over. You are grown now, you had an uneasy transition to adulthood, and you feel like you let the child in yourself die. You killed the child Kori when you became the adult Kori."

Kori looked again at the certificate on the wall. She couldn't really read it from this distance; where had she gotten it? This doctor was really kind of wacky herself.

"If you would like to schedule another session, we can begin to work out this problem you have. We'll have you sleeping again in no time. I don't think it will take more than six or eight sessions for you to find closure. Is this a good time for you, next week? Oh, no, I usually have Mr. Bonkers. What about Monday mornings at 10:00?"

"No, that's not good for me," Kori said, knowing that no time would be good for her to come back here. This lady couldn't help her. She was sure of that.

"Well, do you want some chocolate chip cookies?" Dr. Killingsworth asked, pulling a huge platter of large cookies from beneath a coffee table.

"No, thanks," Kori answered.

"My mother baked them, and she put in extra chunks of chocolate."

"Sounds good, but no, thank you," Kori said. She just wanted to get out of here as soon as she could.

"They are really delicious," the doctor said, taking a huge bite from a huge cookie.

"I'm sure they are," Kori said, feeling full just watching her eat.

"You really should have one, at least one," the doctor begged. "Do you have an eating disorder?" A smear of chocolate clung to her cheek, beside her mouth.

"No, I..." Kori just wanted to leave. "I'm allergic to chocolate," she lied. Why did she say that? She had to say that, because she wasn't allowed to say, 'watching a fat person stuff food in her mouth makes me sick.'

"Oh! Well, there's another possibility we can explore," Dr. Killingsworth said, shoving the rest of the cookie in her mouth. "Here, take my card and give me a call when you know when will be the best time for you to come and see me. We can plan on at least eight to twelve sessions, and after that, if you are not as good as new, we can schedule some more to work on your other issues."

"Okay," Kori said, knowing she would never call, and she would never come here again.

"In the mean time, do you want me to write you a prescription for some sleeping pills?" Dr. Killingsworth asked.

"Oh, no, thank you," Kori said. "I'm allergic to pills."

"I can recommend a good allergy specialist," Dr. Killingsworth suggested.

"Thank you, I already have one," she said, another lie slipping through her lips. When had she become such a liar? She hurriedly got to the door before Dr. Killingsworth could pull herself out of the chair.

"Thanks again," Kori called, as she quickly left the doctor's office and hurried out the front door.

Although Kori hadn't received any help with her nightmare situation, she did feel a lot better about herself, knowing that her problems could be solved, somehow; but that doctor had very serious problems. At least when Kori awakened from her nightmares, she wasn't obese. She glanced at the card the doctor had given her and noticed on the back was the list of fees, which started at $120. per hour and increased from there, depending on the type of therapy. Kori stuck the card in her pocket so she could put it in the trash as soon as she got home. Even if she thought the doctor could help her, Kori could not afford to come to many sessions. Well, she knew Dr. Killingsworth couldn't help her, so the cost not paid was not important. She was so glad the introductory session had been free, with no obligation to ever come for another session.

She still had nearly two hours before she had to go to the station, so she drove home.

CHAPTER 24

"Hey, Kori!" Theo called, as soon as she stepped out of her car. He was at his post, standing on his balcony like the neighborhood sentinel.

"Hi, Theo," she called.

"How's your head?" he asked.

How did he know she had been to a psychiatrist? She hadn't mentioned it to anyone besides Maureen. Could she have announced it on the news? No, Kori was just going crazy... no, she wasn't going crazy, she was just over-tired from lack of sleep! That shrink couldn't help her at all.

"Fine," she answered, not wanting to talk about her visit to Dr. Killingsworth.

"Did the lump go down?"

"Lump?" she asked. Oh, yes, he was talking about the lump on her forehead! "It doesn't hurt at all," she said.

"Do you want to come over for brunch?" he asked. "It's not too early for an early lunch... and it's not to late for a late breakfast; but it's too late for an early breakfast and it's too early for a late lunch."

"No, thanks, I need to get ready for work," she answered.

"How about that glass of lemonade?" Mother Florence asked. She was coming up the sidewalk behind Kori. "The rain check."

Kori needed to be more friendly with her neighbors, and she really did have enough time to visit with them now.

"That sounds swell," she said. Did she just use the word 'swell'? Well, that was what she meant, even if she had never used that word before in her life.

"Well, come on in, Dear," Mother Florence said. She had a calm, serene look on her face, and her voice was so soothing, like Kori's grandmother's voice. "You come on over, too, Theophilis."

"Yes, ma'am!" he said excitedly. Kori wondered where he got all his energy and enthusiasm.

When Kori entered Mother Florence's apartment, she felt a sense of peace flow over her. Frilly cloths adorned all the flat surfaces, and beautiful flowers were everywhere – but the place didn't seem cluttered. It was just lovely. They sat around a small table and Mother Florence served lemonade.

"I hope you are feeling much better today," she said to Kori.

"Oh, yes, I am," she said. She had decided to put the visit to the wacky quack out of her mind, and not to mention it to anyone – ever.

"That was quite a nasty bump you received," Theo said.

"Yep," Kori said, trying to forget about that also.

"Sometimes we can have pain deep on the inside that affects us on the outside," Mother Florence said.

Kori looked at her suspiciously.

"Sometimes the answers to our problems can be found in unexpected places," Mother Florence said. "We don't know the answers. We can be stuck with a problem for months or years, and have no idea that the solution is right in front of us."

What was she saying? Did she know something about Kori's situation?

"My Dear, have you taken it to the Lord in prayer?" she asked.

"What?"

"Your problem; have you taken it to the Lord in prayer?"

"Why would I do that?" Kori asked.

"He knows all about it," Mother Florence answered.

"All about it?"

"The Lord knows your thoughts before you think them; and still, He loves you. He wants you to bring your problems to Him."

"Why?"

"So He can show you the solutions. He's the only One who can help you."

"How do you know I need help?"

"Oh, my Dear, we all need help from the Lord. None of us can do it all ourselves. What are we, but wretched sinners? We can't do anything without Him."

"I've been doing everything myself, without Him. He doesn't really care about me."

"He *does* care. And if you have been doing everything without Him, that is your problem right there. We need God. He doesn't need us."

"Why would He care about me?"

"He loves you so much, He sent His only Son to die for you, for your sins, in your place."

"I've heard that; John 3:16, right? God loves the world so much, He gave His only Son."

"It's not the earth He loves – it's all the people in the world. He made us in His image, to have fellowship with Him and to love Him. He wants us to love Him – but He won't force us to love Him. He wants us to choose to love Him. He wants us to accept His Son, Jesus. No matter what else we do in our lives, He wants to know what we will do with His Son. Will we accept Him, or will we reject Him?"

"I thought God wanted us to live good lives and be nice to people and be honest and stuff," Kori said. She noticed that Theo was oddly silent.

"God knows that we can't be good; that's why He wants us to accept Jesus and the Gift of the Holy Spirit."

"Wait – if we can't be good, how can anyone get into heaven?"

"We don't get to heaven on our own merit, we get to heaven by believing in Jesus. It's not what we do, it's what we believe. In God's eyes, there are only two types of people in the world: those who believe in His Son, Jesus, and those who do not believe in Jesus."

Kori had never heard that before. She had thought there were all kinds of people in the world. Mother Florence seemed to read her mind.

"People will make all kinds of distinctions between people, but to God, there are only believers in Jesus and non-believers in Jesus. The wonderful thing is, any non-believer can become a believer. It's an individual choice. God can help you with everything in your life, but you have to make that choice for yourself."

Kori wondered if God could help with her problem. She hadn't thought to ask Him; but was her problem too insignificant to Him? She felt tears behind her eyes.

"God gave us a Gift: His Son, Jesus," Mother Florence said. "And within the Gift of His Son, He gave other gifts: forgiveness of sin, salvation, comfort from the Holy Spirit, eternal life, hope, peace, joy, love, and the list goes on. Do you need some peace of mind today?"

Kori nodded. Maybe her answer was in God.

"Do you feel something within yourself, something drawing you nearer to God?"

Kori nodded again. She was afraid to use her voice.

121

"That is the Holy Spirit of God, tugging at your heart. If you feel God is speaking to you today, you can accept His Son, Jesus, right now, and be saved."

"Saved?" Kori whispered. "From what?"

"You will be saved from sin and death; you will receive eternal life today. Do you feel it? Is God speaking to your heart?"

"Yes," Kori said softly.

"The Bible tells us that we all have sinned and come short of the glory of God. Do you know that you are a sinner? Oh, it's okay. I am too. Everyone is. But God wants us to admit it."

Kori thought about the lies she had been telling lately. Yes, she was a sinner. She was a liar, and that meant she was a sinner.

"I'm a sinner," she admitted. She felt tears running down her face, but she didn't care. She DID need God. She had lived her own life without Him for so long, and she was so tired. She needed Him to take care of her. "Forgive me, God, for everything. I didn't know what I was doing. Wait – I knew what I was doing, I just didn't know how bad it was. I'm really a bad person, aren't I?"

"Do you believe that Jesus died on the cross for your sins, all of your sins?"

"Yes," Kori said with relief. Maybe God could take care of her nightmares.

"Your sins are forgiven. All you had to do was ask Him for forgiveness. Dying on the cross wasn't all Jesus did for you," Mother Florence said tenderly. "He died on the cross, and He was placed in a tomb, but on the third day, He rose from the dead, defeating death, proving that He is the Son of God. Do you believe that He is the Son of God, and that He rose from the dead on the third day?"

"I have heard that before, but I didn't really understand it until now," Kori admitted. "I believe it."

"The Holy Spirit is opening your understanding right now. The Bible tells us in the book of Romans, chapter 10, if you confess with your mouth the Lord Jesus, and you believe in your heart that God raised Him from the dead, you shall be saved. You just confessed that you believe, so you are saved! You are now a child of God and you can take your problems to Him. He will help you.

"I also am willing to help you with anything, just ask," Mother Florence added.

"Me too, Kori, whatever you need, just ask," Theo said, grinning. "You're saved!"

"Forgive me, God, for everything!" Kori said.

"Let's join our hands in prayer," Mother Florence said. "Our Father in heaven, thank You for this child, leading her here on this morning so she could get to know You and accept Your Son, Jesus. Now, Lord, protect her and guide her by Your Holy Spirit. In the name of Jesus we pray. Amen."

"Amen," Kori said. "Oh, I need to get to work! What time is it?"

"Almost eleven," Mother Florence said.

"Is that all? Wow, it seems like I've been here for hours," Kori said.

"God stretched out time so you could get what you need," Theo said.

"And Jesus will always be with you, from this moment on," Mother Florence said. "He will never leave you alone. He gave His promise."

"Thank you, both, so much," Kori said as she rose to leave. "Oh, my lemonade!" She hadn't touched it, so now she finished it as she stood beside the table. She felt strangely comforted – which, she noted, was not the same as feeling comfortable – just being in the presence of these two caring people. She sensed that they really did care about her, about the person inside of her, not for what they could get from her or what she could do for them, but just because they cared... similar to the way God cared for her.

She knew God cared for her. As she left Mother Florence's apartment and returned to her own apartment, she knew without a doubt that God did care for her, and that He was happy about the choice she had just made, to accept His Son, Jesus. She felt better than she had felt in years, but the feeling was somewhat familiar. She was reminded of when she was a child and had gotten in trouble, and she felt like she had to hide from her parents, or she couldn't be completely open with them, because she had a secret from them; then when her parents discovered what she had done, they had been angry at her for a minute, or an hour, but after they had confronted her and she had confessed, then her parents let her know they really did love her anyway. After it was all over, she felt closer to them than before, because she didn't have a barrier, even within her own mind, between herself and her parents. They knew her and what she had done, and they still loved her even though they knew she wasn't perfect. Coming to God made her feel the same way: He knew every terrible thing she had done, but He loved her and He accepted her anyway, and now they had no barrier between them, the barrier she had created. She felt a warmth engulf her, from the inside of her heart, all the way to the outermost part of her skin. She was tingling all over her head and neck.

As she got ready to go to work, she realized that she didn't feel as tired as she had all week. She felt rested! She finally felt as if she were no longer struggling against the current; she was no longer striving against God, but now she was going along with Him. Her whole burden was lifted, because she stopped resisting the tugging of God, and just accepted Him.

The doctor hadn't helped her at all this morning. She wondered, to whom did the doctor go for help? She was truly in need of some help. Kori realized that the doctor needed God, too, as much as she did.

CHAPTER 25

When she arrived at the station, Jim Smith was sitting in his usual position, leaning back in his chair, his fingers interlaced behind his head. He was at work, but he was not doing any work. Kori didn't feel irritated by him today. She didn't care if he didn't like her. She knew God loved her. She smiled as she took over the board from Brad.

"My, aren't we happy today?" Brad asked.

"Yes, we are," Kori replied. "Are you happy? I am happy."

"Did you take your happy pills today?" Jim Smith asked.

"No, I did not," Kori said.

"Oh, that's right, didn't you go to a shrink this morning?" Jim Smith asked. How did he know about that? Kori had thought that was confidential information, but obviously, in a news department, nothing was confidential. Everything about everybody was news.

"I did go to a doctor, but just for a short visit, and I won't be going back to her again," Kori said.

"Are you crazy?" Jim Smith asked.

"Smitty, you don't ask someone who stopped going to a shrink if they are crazy!" Brad said. "I mean, you don't ask a crazy person if they are crazy, and you don't ask someone who stopped going to a shrink if they are crazy, because, do you mean are they crazy and that's why they went, or are they crazy and that's why they stopped going?"

"Huh?" Jim Smith asked.

"Never mind," Brad said. "Obviously, Kori is the sane one and you are the one who is crazy."

"So, why is Kori so happy?" Jim Smith asked. "She looks like a different person."

Kori felt like a different person. She wasn't bothered that he was looking at her or making remarks about her. He wasn't bothering her at all today, and she knew that nothing he said or did would be able to take away the peace she felt inside of her. The calm within her mind was hers to keep forever.

"Kori, I would tell you to have a nice day," Brad said, "but I can see you already are." He slipped through the door to the engineering room.

"Doncha just love Danny DiVito?" Jim Smith asked.

"Not really," Kori answered. She didn't really think of him one way or another.

"He's so hilarious, he just cracks me up, you know what I mean?"

"I guess," she said, just to be nice. She knew he was trying to start an argument, but it was so trivial. She would do better to just agree instead of fighting with him.

"What about Arnold? Doncha just love Arnold?" Jim Smith asked.

"Arnold?" she asked, not sure who he meant. "Yeah, he's all right."

"Did you watch 'Idol' last night?" he asked, happy to have a conversation.

"No, I was working," she said, "and it's on another channel."

"Oh, that's right," he said, then, without pausing, "well, you should have seen it, there was this one guy, he was really good, and everyone thought he should win, you know what I mean, he was really good, and he had a lot of votes and everything, and everyone thought he had it tied up, you know what I mean, then this one chick, a really hot chick came on, I guess she was on before but I missed it last week because I was moving and I couldn't even set up to record it, so she was really hot, you know what I mean, and she came on, and she just blew everyone out of the water, you know what I mean?"

"Really?" Kori had no idea what he meant.

"So she came on and she sang that song, oh, you know, you've heard it, it's really popular right now, but it's a remake of one of those songs from the 70's, you know, do you know which one I'm talking about?"

"I'm not sure," Kori said, wondering how Jim Smith could ever actually communicate with anyone.

"Well, it goes like, well, you know, I can't sing it, but she came on, and she was dressed really fine, you know, and she came on, and she just belted it right out and she blew everyone away, right off the map, and, like, no one was expecting it from her, since she came out dressed in a bikini, you know, that didn't hurt her at all, as a matter of fact, it was quite enhancing to her performance, and she just blew them all away, you know what I mean? So then, everyone thought she had it, like, she was clearly the best, she beat the others hands down, you know what I mean, and then, like, she didn't win! I was floored! I could not believe it! No one could! You know what I mean? And, like, the guy didn't win either, but some dude from Texas won, like, his brother was one of the judges or something, like, he wasn't even in the running, he was so far behind, and then, like he pulls something out of the hat like this, you know what I mean?"

Kori had never seen the program, so she did not know what he meant. However, instead of being irritated by his ramblings, Kori was rather amused. He was kind of funny, even in his ignorance. Kori's whole attitude about him was different. She even felt kind of sorry for him.

"So are you going to Cracker's going away party tonight?" he asked.

"I'm working tonight," she answered.

"Well, so is everyone who is anyone, but the party will still be going on long after you drones get off work. That is what I love about this shift! It is so excellent, you know what I mean? Nine to five-thirty, weekends off, man! This is the life! I mean, I can really get into this! You know what I mean? I go home, put on a movie, have a few beers, put on another movie, and drink myself to sleep, every night. Then I wake up the next day and do it all again. This is the coolest, you know what I mean? Kori? What has gotten into you?"

"God," she answered softly.

"What? What's the matter? Are you okay?"

"I'm fine. I have God inside of me. Today I accepted Jesus. That is why I am different now."

"Oh, man, you're not going to become one of those religious freaks, are you? You're not gonna be walking around with a sign that says 'the end is near,' and giving up TV and everything, are you?"

"I don't know what I am going to do, but I know what I have already done, and today, my life has been changed."

"The shrink made you accept Jesus? Whoa!"

"No, I went to the doctor and realized that she couldn't help me. I think her problems were worse than mine. Then when I went home, one of my neighbors introduced me to Jesus."

127

"Male or female?"

"Jesus is a man, you know that, don't you?"

"No, I mean, your neighbor, male or female?"

"Actually, one man and one lady."

"Did they brainwash you or something? Are you in a cult now?"

"No, I just accepted Jesus, and they are really nice people."

"Yeah, everyone needs some really nice people in their lives, you know what I mean?"

"As a matter of fact, I do know what you mean, and these are really nice people."

At that moment, Rose came charging in from the newsroom.

"You won't believe it!" she shouted, out of breath. "Maureen just went into labor and Buddy took her to the hospital! So I'm going to be sitting in for her this evening!"

"She's just about a week early, isn't she?" Kori asked.

"If you ask me, she was ready to pop," Jim Smith said.

"We didn't ask you, James," Rose said. "Anyway, that's not all. You know Jerry, who does the early show? His wife is also in the hospital, and she just had a baby boy this morning."

"Oh, that's right!" Kori said. "She was due a couple of weeks ago, wasn't she?"

"Eleven days, and last night she went into labor," Rose said. "And you know that Jeff's wife is due to have a baby today, right? She just went into labor also, so Jeff's taking her to the hospital – and there's more!"

"You're kidding!" Jim Smith said.

"Do I look like I'm kidding?" Rose asked.

"No, you look very serious right now," he answered.

"I am. Rob's wife also went into labor last night, and she's in the hospital too. Her baby is almost a month early, but so far, she is fine."

"I can't believe it, four babies added to our little family in one day?" Kori asked.

"Well, here's the topper," Rose said. "Ken's wife is also in the hospital having a baby."

"When it rains, it pours," Jim Smith said.

"I didn't even know he was married," Kori said.

"Neither did any of his girlfriends," Rose said.

128

"Girlfriends?" Jim Smith asked.

Rose ignored him. "So I'll be doing the news this evening, and Danny will do the sports and I guess Tom will come in to do the weather. I hope by news time I can announce five new babies on our news team! That has to be some kind of a record! No other station in town will have news like that today, or in the country, for that matter!"

"That is really a miracle," Jim Smith said. "So many new babies born in one day!"

Kori was thinking that the miracle was not the five new babies being born today, but the real miracle was that she had been born again today.

"So, are you guys going to the party for Cracker tonight?" Rose asked.

"I wouldn't miss it for the world," Jim Smith said.

"I don't know," Kori said. She was looking forward to finally getting some sleep, confident that God had taken care of her nightmare problem, so she didn't want to be up very late tonight.

"Come on, it'll be fun," Rose said, "a real celebration."

"Rosie, are you nervous about doing the news?" Jim Smith asked.

"A woman has to do what a woman has to do," Rose said, smiling.

"Hey, yeah, this is your big break, you know what I mean?" Jim Smith said.

"As a matter of fact, I DO know what you mean," Rose said, suddenly serious.

"What do you mean?" Jim Smith asked.

She burst into laughter. "I'm just teasing you," she said.

"You better watch it," he warned. "I heard what you did to Snorty, and you better not try that with me."

"What?" Rose asked innocently.

"That trick you played, about your car."

"It wasn't a trick, he just wasn't thinking," Kori said.

"Well, you're not going to catch me thinking, you know what I mean?"

"I know what you mean," Rose said, leaving the control room.

"IT'S A BOY!" an announcer said over the station's loud speaker. "Maureen and Buddy are the proud parents of a ten-and-a-half pound baby boy!"

"Wow, they just made it to the hospital in time," Kori said.

"Buddy, Junior," Jim Smith said.

"What?"

"That's what they are going to name him, after his dad."

"I thought Buddy was a nickname or something," Kori said.

"Nope. He had his name legally changed when he turned 18," Jim Smith explained. "I would have, too, if I had his old name."

"Why, what was his name?"

"You're going to laugh," Jim Smith predicted.

"Why, what was his name?" Kori repeated.

Jim Smith started laughing. His face turned dark red as he laughed himself right out of his chair. From the floor, he could just barely say it: "Constantine."

"What? What kind of name is that?"

"A funny one!" Jim Smith said, between breaths of air. "Of course, you can guess what his nickname was, you know what I mean?"

"No, what?" Kori asked.

"You can't guess?"

"No, what was it?"

"It's so obvious."

"What was it?"

"You're going to crack up."

"What was it?"

"Okay – are you ready?"

"Yes!"

"His nickname was..." Jim Smith was laughing so hard, it seemed as if he would never stop. "It was...Constipation!"

Kori didn't think it was very funny, but then, the type of humor the guys at the station liked wasn't always funny to her.

"So do you understand why he wanted to change his name to Buddy?" Jim Smith asked.

"Yes, I understand," Kori said.

That afternoon, with the last minute substitutions, including Prather taking Jeff's place, Tom taking Rob's place, Danny taking Buddy's place, and Rose, who did a beautiful job her first time as news anchor, the news went incredibly well. At the end of the newscast, Rose announced the birth of five new babies, three girls and two boys, in one day, to parents who worked on the news team.

Jim Smith turned to Kori as soon as he had made the switch to join with the network programming and raised his hand to give her a high-five. Kori thought it was incredibly corny, but she was in such a good mood, she returned the gesture and slapped his hand, recognizing that this was the first time they had ever made contact with each other. His hand was really sweaty.

CHAPTER 26

Kori went home to have dinner and thought about the extraordinary events of the day. She had gone to a psychiatrist who needed more help than she did; she had visited with two neighbors who introduced her to God and His Son, Jesus, and her life made a noticeable turn, right then and there; she had not had a conflict at work with Jim Smith; and five babies had been born to her co-workers at the TV station. The best news was, after five nights of nightmares and sleeplessness, and five days of being overtired, irritated and exhausted, she was going to get some rest tonight – as soon as she came home from the party, which she really didn't want to attend, but she would go anyway, for a short time.

As she relaxed after dinner on the couch with Tundra, thoughts of Paul Pardo popped into her head. She had settled things with God, and He accepted her, failures and all. Now she needed to settle things with Paul. She had always felt that he had driven her away from him, and because of his selfish attitude, she had refused to speak to him ever again. She had never had any desire to contact him. She had gone through enough suffering by herself – she didn't want to include him or share any of it with him. After all, it had been completely his fault; she had had to endure the affliction on her own. God had punished her for her involvement, all those years ago. Now she was free from all that – but she needed to forgive Paul. She needed to let him know that she had forgiven him.

She wondered if he had ever gotten married? He would have been a fine catch for anyone who loved a smart, handsome, kind, generous, soft-spoken type of man. He had made it clear to Kori that she wasn't quite up to his level, that she was a person who made mistakes, and he didn't. When she ended their relationship, she was relieved to think that he would never know the extent of her inadequacies. He would never know what a bad person she was.

Today, things were different. She had been a bad person, and she now could admit it – because now she was forgiven. She had been forgiven by God, so she could also forgive Paul. She closed her eyes and asked God to let her forgive him, to let him go completely. In some subconscious part of her mind, she knew why she had never dated since their relationship had ended: she was still holding on to him, and she felt that no other man would ever measure up to his standards. He was such a great guy, but he was too great for her. Now she could be free to accept a man on her own level; a man who also loved God the way she did, so they could share their faith in God together.

She began to doze and as she did, she stepped right back into the nightmare. She was sitting in a courtroom, like the ones on Matlock or Perry Mason, but she didn't have a famous attorney with her to plead her case. The judge was reading off the list of charges, but he was speaking in another language, until he got to the last line, which he spoke in plain English.

"...charged with murder in the first degree. How do you plead?"

His voice was strikingly familiar. That was a voice she had known and loved for a long time – a long time ago. She couldn't see him at first - he was sitting in the shadows - but she knew who he was. She opened her mouth to answer, but her throat was so dry, she couldn't respond. Her lips moved soundlessly. The entire group in the courtroom began to surround her; even the walls began to get closer to her and she felt like she just couldn't get a breath of air. She was so very hot.

"She has been forgiven," she heard another voice say. She didn't see the Person who spoke, but she knew who He was. He hadn't left her alone! He had promised to be with her always, and here He was, to defend her! She awakened with a huge sense of relief, with Tundra asleep on her chest, crushing her and heating her. Kori smiled as she prepared to return to the station for her late shift.

CHAPTER 27

The station was buzzing with excitement when Kori arrived. Everybody was excited about the new babies and the party, which had already started. Most of the news team had visited the hospital, and they returned with surprising news: Ken was asking for a transfer out of state to a sister station. He didn't want to return to the news set because Rose had announced on the air the birth of his daughter, along with the other four babies who had been born today. The station had received numerous calls for him, and at the hospital he had been visited by several women, all who claimed to be his fiancé. They had been shocked to hear that he was married and that his wife just had a baby. He had taken advantage of his good looks, and now his infidelity was completely exposed, both at work and to his wife.

"Got caught with his hand in the proverbial cookie jar," Snorty remarked.

"Do you think God has a sense of humor?" Kori asked.

"Oh, yes, indeed!" Snorty replied. "But more importantly, He has a sense of righteousness, and what a man reaps, that will he sow. It's a known fact."

"Don't you mean he will reap what he sows?"

"Yeah, isn't that what I said? That's what I meant."

"Do you go to church?" Kori asked, realizing that after working with him all these years, she had no idea what Snorty did on weekends.

"Yes, I do," he said, looking around to be sure no one else was listening. He lowered his voice. "Every Sunday I go to that little church right next to Domino's Pizza, with my mother. Don't tell anyone."

Kori realized that even though he was kind of weird, he loved God too.

CHAPTER 28

After the late news, Kori and Rose went together to the party. They rode in Kori's car because it was too cold and dark to ride in a convertible. Rob had predicted tomorrow would be a sunny day; they could enjoy Rose's car then.

As soon as they stepped into the house, Kori wished she hadn't come. A sickening smell of alcohol hung in the room, and several people were smoking. She didn't want to be near drinkers or smokers. She followed Rose, the forever-smiling Rose, into the kitchen. A small lady she didn't know was standing in the kitchen, holding a tea bag. Kori's eyes were drawn to her and she couldn't stop staring at her. The lady pulled the tea bag out of its wrapper and she began to sniff it. She kept sniffing the bag, and that annoyed Kori. Kori kept watching her. Why didn't she stop smelling the tea bag? Wasn't one sniff enough?

Kori followed Rose to the dining room where Rose began talking to some of the news team. Kori stayed for a moment. Her eyes were irritated by the thick smoke in the room. She left Rose and stepped through the sliding glass door, onto the patio, and inhaled the fresh air.

"Kori!" Jim Smith shouted, as if he were happy to see her. "You finally made it!"

Kori could tell he had been drinking. He and Brad were sitting at a picnic table with a dozen empty beer bottles in front of them. She walked over to the table and sat across from them.

"Have a beer!" Brad said, raising a bottle.

"No, thanks, I don't like beer," Kori said.

"Ya just hafta get used to it," Jim Smith said, slurring his words.

"I don't want to get used to it, and besides, I'm the designated driver."

"Will you drive me home?" Jim Smith asked, grinning, turning his head sideways, like a puppy would.

"I'm not going to drive you home," Kori said. "Why would I drive a person home who hates me?" Oops, she hadn't meant to say that. Maybe he wouldn't remember she had said that when he was sober.

"Hate you? I don't hate you," Jim Smith said. "You're the one who hates me."

"I do not hate you!" Kori protested. "I don't hate anybody!"

"But you hate me," he said, looking kind of sad.

"No, I don't hate you," she said.

"Well, I don't hate you, but I thought you hated me."

"Why would you think I hate you?" she asked.

"The first day I came back to work, Snorty told me, you hate me."

"What?" Kori asked, stunned. "He told me, YOU hate ME!"

"How could I hate you? I didn't even know you."

"I know! That's what I told him! But he said you hated me!"

"He told me you hated me because I stole your job."

"He told ME you hated ME because I stole YOUR job!"

"So," Brad said slowly, "you two have merely been pawns in Snorty's game of living chess."

"That's a good one, you know what I mean?" Jim Smith asked, snickering.

"That's what it is," Brad said, matter-of-factly.

"Well, we should celebrate," Jim Smith said. "Let's have another beer."

Nobody moved.

"Bradly, would you be so kind as to get us another beer?" Jim Smith asked.

"You get your own beer, Smitty," Brad said. "I still have half a bottle. And get your hand off my leg."

Jim Smith looked at Kori. "You can just call me Roscoe."

"Roscoe? Why would I call you Roscoe?" she asked.

"Just because." He smiled at her with dull eyes.

"I'm not going to call you Roscoe."

"Why not?"

"It's not your name."

"You can still call me Roscoe."

"I don't think so."

"Why not?"

"I think I have to go now," Kori said.

"You just got here!" Brad said.

"The party's just starting!" Jim Smith added.

"It seems to be coming to an end, for me," she said.

"Who'd you come here with?" Brad asked.

"Rose."

Jim Smith was suddenly perky.

"Down, Boy!" Brad said.

"Rose? Rose is here?" Jim Smith asked, looking around the patio. He sat up straight, reminding Kori of a meerkat. His head turned quickly to the left and right as he searched for her.

"She's in the kitchen," Kori said.

"Maybe she can give me a ride home," he said.

"She rode with me," Kori said,

"No, I mean, maybe she can drive my car home," he explained. "I can't be driving tonight."

"The last time Smitty went driving after drinking, he hit a parked car," Brad said, "with a riding lawn mower."

"Two," Jim Smith corrected, giggling like a girl.

"Two parked cars, two days in jail," Brad explained. He nodded his head introspectively.

Kori thought about people getting what they deserved. She had deserved terrible punishment for her sins, but God had forgiven her. Snorty had set up two people to hate each other, and now he was alone, at work at the TV station, while the rest of the staff was celebrating at the party (except those who were celebrating at the hospital.) What did Paul Pardo deserve, after sending her away from him? Did she deserve to spend the rest of her life without him, the only man she had ever loved?

"Kori, do you want to stay?" Rose asked, breaking into her thoughts.

"Not really," Kori said, "but I'll stay until you're ready to go."

"Hi, Rose!" Jim Smith said excitedly.

"Hi, James; good-bye, James," she said. "Hi, Brad."

"Wanna sit with us?" Jim Smith asked.

"Actually, I'm ready to go now, if you are, Kori," Rose said. "I've had a really long day, and another long one tomorrow."

"Me, too," Kori agreed. They left the party while it was in full swing. Kori took Rose back to the station to get her car. As soon as Rose started her car, Kori left her and drove home.

When she was ready to settle into bed with Tundra, Kori began to think about God. He knew everything, He saw everything, and even if it seemed like He wasn't taking care of things, He really was, in His own way. He was the Judge and He would decide what everyone deserved. Kori didn't have to think about it – she could just let Him take care of everything.

Tundra made herself comfortable on Kori's head and began to bathe herself. Kori wanted to relax, but her head was being jarred with each movement.

"Tundra, stop!" Kori said.

Tundra stopped... for a few seconds, then she started again.

"Tundra! If you're going to do that, you have to move!"

Tundra paused again, then she resumed her grooming.

"It's bad enough that I let you sleep on my pillow and on my head. You don't have to take a bath right here, right now!" Kori reached up to move her cat off her head and Tundra bit her hand.

"Ow! Tundy, don't do that!"

Tundra got mad and jumped off the bed. She would be back in a few minutes. Kori nuzzled her head into her pillow and she was instantly asleep.

CHAPTER 29

Kori was guilty. She had been forgiven, but she was still guilty. She had tried to keep her secret, but everybody knew it. The odd thing was, she couldn't remember her secret, her crime, but she knew everyone was condemning her. How could she be guilty and forgiven at the same time? Did that mean she would escape punishment, but everyone would hate her?

Somebody didn't hate her. A misunderstanding had caused all the problems. She had kept secrets and closed doors. She had blamed others, but it had really been all her fault. She didn't know what to do.

She remembered that she was not alone. Somebody was on her side. Somebody cared for her. Somebody knew the truth about her and He still loved her. She didn't have to face her trial alone. All she needed to do was to ask for help.

She was unable to open her mouth to ask for help. Her lips were sealed shut. They felt like they had wax on them. She couldn't speak! How could she ask for the help she needed?

He knew her thoughts. All she had to do was to think. She couldn't think! Her mind was stalled! No words would form in her mind!

Help me, she thought. Please, help me.

She didn't know what she needed or what was the solution, but she rested in the fact that He knew what she needed and He knew what to do. He could and would help her. She breathed a sigh of relief.

SATURDAY
CHAPTER 30

Rose came to get Kori at noon so they could go for a drive in her new car. The sun was shining brightly and the day was perfect for riding in Rose's convertible. Rose warned Kori to either tie her hair in a pony tail or wear a scarf, to avoid major tangles when they finished their ride. Kori pulled her curls back into a pony tail since she didn't have a scarf, and they got into Rose's car. Rose was wearing a fashionable scarf.

"Do you want to ride up to Grand Forks?" Rose asked.

"What's in Grand Forks?"

"I don't know, cute guys?"

"Anyone in particular?"

"Maybe."

"Let's go. I just have to be back by 5:00."

"Yeah, me too."

They rode through town, smiling at everyone who paid attention to this nice-looking new car. Rose got on the freeway to Grand Forks.

"I went to see Maureen this morning," Rose said.

"How is she? Did you see the baby?"

"I saw all five babies. They are so darling! Buddy, Jr. is the biggest. Maureen is doing really well. She's so relieved. He's so cute."

"What about the other babies?"

"Jerry's and Rob's daughters are kind of small, but the others looked really big, especially Buddy Junior. He has a head full of red hair, just like his daddy."

"Buddy got his little football player," Kori remarked.

"Yeah, and he looks like he's about the size to start playing next year!"

"Now Maureen will have two sports fans at home."

"Wasn't that weird about Ken?" Rose asked. "I mean, I didn't know he had all those girlfriends who didn't know about his wife. I wouldn't have announced it on the news if I had known. Well, maybe I would have announced it, I mean, it really was news, five babies born on the same day. But how could I have known?"

"No one knew, I guess, not his wife or any of his girlfriends."

"Wow, you never know who is living a secret life," Rose remarked.

Jim Smith had a secret life... working by day and going home every evening and watching movies and drinking himself to sleep; how many people knew about his drinking problem and his time in jail? Snorty had a secret life... working all night and then secretly going to church on Sundays with his mother. Kori had known him all these years and she never knew he went to church. Why did he keep it a secret? Was he afraid he would be teased?

Kori thought about her life, how once it seemed enticing to live a secret life, where no one knew her or her family, and no one knew her past. She had thought of it as a fresh start, a clean slate, with acceptance and no judgment. She had established herself here, in North Dakota. She had new friends, a good reputation at her job, a reputation she built herself, by her own hard work and dedication. She had a past here, a past that included nothing of which she needed to be ashamed; and now she had another fresh start just yesterday, living her life with and for God, and not just for herself, and not by herself.

"There's a guy in Grand Forks," Rose confessed.

"What a surprise," Kori said knowingly.

"His name is Travis, and he's really nice. He works at the University. I met him when I did a story a couple of months ago, actually, the first news story I did."

"And?" Kori asked.

"And I just want to stop by and say hi, then we can go back home," Rose said, "if that's okay with you."

"It's your car," Kori said, "and you're driving. I'm just a passenger, along for the ride, which, by the way, is very enjoyable."

"Thank you," Rose said, as she took the exit to Grand Forks.

"Does he know you're coming?"

"No, I wanted to surprise him."

Kori wondered if Rose were trying to check on him, to see what he would be doing if he didn't know she was coming to see him, but she dismissed the thought. Rose's motives weren't that significant to her, but her friendship was very significant.

Rose drove to a nice area in town and stopped in front of some new condos.

"Come on, let's go in," she said. "You have to meet Travis."

Just as Kori was getting out of the car, an extremely handsome man came out of one of the condos.

"Is that him?" Kori whispered.

"That's him," Rose said, beaming.

"Rosebud!" he shouted when he saw her. "What a surprise! What are you doing here? I would have fixed some lunch for us if I had known you were coming!"

"Surprise!" Rose said, pattering up the sidewalk to meet him. He swung her around in a circle, lifting her feet off the ground as they hugged. "I just wanted you to meet my friend, Kori. Kori, this is Travis."

"Nice to meet you, Kori," he said. "And I really like your car."

"Nice meeting you too, but it's not mine – it's Rose's car," Kori said.

"You got a new car?" he asked, astonished. "That is beautiful! You mentioned you were looking at cars, but I didn't know you bought one already! It's you! It fits you perfectly! I wouldn't have chosen any other car for you – it's yours! This car was made for you!" He circled the car, examining it.

"This was the one that jumped out and said 'buy me,' so I did," Rose explained.

"I can see why! This car was made just for you! It's lovely," Travis said.

"Are you going somewhere?" Rose asked. "We can't stay anyway. I just needed to get some freeway miles on my new car."

"I was just going to meet some of the other faculty members so we can practice for the student-staff baseball game. You can come and watch, if you want."

"No, we need to get back. We both have to work this evening, but I just wanted to come up and--"

"You are welcome to come any time, you know that. Come back in two weeks, when we have the game. I would be honored to have you here cheering for me."

"If I don't have to work, I will come," Rose promised.

"Oh, Rosebud, I caught you on the news yesterday," Travis said. "You were wonderful! And that thing at the end about all the babies born at your station in one day, was that true?"

"It has to be true. It was on the news," Rose said, smiling.

"Hmmm, it wasn't April Fool's Day or anything, was it?" Travis said.

"Tomorrow is Mother's Day," Kori said.

"Well, there you go, five new mothers in one day!" Rose said.

"I'm going to be down your way in a few days," Travis said. "I'm going to be doing a lecture there."

"I'll be sure to get tickets," Rose said. She hadn't stopped smiling all afternoon.

"I have a seat reserved for you already, in the front row," Travis said, winking at her. "You're the press, aren't you? And I hope you'll be off duty, so we can go to dinner before the lecture."

Kori was stung with the memory of when Paul used to wink at her, and she had melted under his gaze. She forced her smile to stay on her face, but she felt herself crying in her heart. That had been so long ago, in another lifetime, when she had been able to freely give and receive love. In this lifetime, the new, clean-slate lifetime, she went to work and she went home, eating and sleeping, loving only Tundra, avoiding any relationship that had the possibility of becoming something close. Yes, she had Jesus in her heart right now, but what she had lost and the love she had eliminated from her life all those years ago was still causing her pain.

Rose and Kori left Grand Forks and returned to the TV station just in time to go to work. Kori felt rather subdued after seeing Rose and her friend, as if she had lost something a long time ago and she needed to find it. She usually liked working on the weekends because the pace was so much more laid-back, with the weekend director, Morehouse, who had the nickname 'Mellowhouse.' However, this evening she wished she had more pressure at work, other thoughts to fill her mind, so she would stop thinking about her past and she could move into her future. The evening passed slowly but smoothly, and Kori was glad to finally go home after work.

CHAPTER 31

Kori was exhausted. Was that just today when she had ridden to Grand Forks with Rose? Or was it about a month ago? The day had seemed so long, and now she could finally rest... or could she? She had come to God and she had accepted Jesus, but she still was having nightmares. She decided to do something she hadn't done since she was a child: she knelt beside her bed to pray. Tundra came to see what she was doing, then, as if in reverence, she crouched and turned her face to the floor.

Kori didn't know how to pray.

"God, I don't know what to say, but I need Your help. You said You would always be with me, and I need You to be with me right now.

"What is going on with me? Why do I keep having these nightmares? I know I was really bad, but that was before, in my old life, a long time ago, and when I came here, I started over with a fresh start. You know that. I've tried to be really good while I was here, and I couldn't even do that. I mean, I wasn't as bad as I was before, but I still wasn't really good. You know all about me and You still love me anyway, and I'm so thankful for that, for Your love and acceptance.

"Please give me some rest and relief. I know You don't want me to be tortured by nightmares for the rest of my life, and I know You don't want me to keep suffering from lack of sleep. I want to be my best for You, so people will look at me and my life and the way I live and they will say, 'She is a person who loves God and her life displays it.' Help me?"

She didn't know what else to say, so she knelt quietly for a few minutes. She felt such a sense of peace come over her, she didn't want to move. Didn't Mother Florence tell her to wait on the Lord, and He would renew her strength?

"Forgive and confess."

Kori turned to see who had said that, but she was the only one in the room besides her cat. Tundra was all huddled like a little bunny, and she certainly hadn't said anything.

Had she heard a voice through the floor or wall of her apartment? Had the voice come from her own mind? Was God speaking to her?

She let God reveal what was deep in her heart. She was ready to forgive Paul for sending her away and causing her to end their relationship, but it was all his fault. What did she have to confess? She felt the pain of guilt gripping her heart. She was not to blame! Their breakup was all his fault!

She had broken ties with her family after she and Paul separated. She didn't want them to know what a terrible person she was, or to think bad things about her. She had left the area for a fresh start so they would never find out her secret.

Was that what she needed to confess? Did she have to tell her parents, and admit what a terrible sinner she had been? The incident happened so many years ago, and she was a different person now... she had to tell them everything. She had to tell them the truth. She couldn't even admit it to herself, but she had to ask God for the courage to tell them... and she had to tell Paul. She had to confess, not only to God, but to Paul AND to her parents. God had already forgiven her, but if she didn't tell them the truth, she could never reconcile with her parents, nor could she ever be truly free from Paul. Her life here, all this time, had really been a life on hold, and now she needed to move forward, advance and grow.

"God, I realize now, You were always watching me. You know what really happened. Ever since college, I blamed Paul for sending me back to Seattle and ending our relationship, but really, it was all my fault. I was the one who ended it. I was the one who made the mistake and I was the one who kept the secret from him all this time. I am a liar and I am a murderer. I know You have forgiven me, but I can't escape the truth of what I did."

CHAPTER 32

Behind Kori's closed eyes, she traveled back in time, to the day she left Paul in Boston, to a time when she said she loved Paul more than anything; but she really loved herself with Paul in her life. Paul had been an enhancement to her life. He made everything in her life better than it was without him. She loved what he added to her life, and their lives had been so easy, so natural together.

The day he forced her to leave, she was so upset. She thought they had become closer to each other during her visit. She had done everything for him, in anticipation of marrying him. She didn't want to go back to Seattle and live the next year and a half without Paul; she just wanted to be with him. He was sending her home. He wasn't ready to be with her all the time. He needed his space, and time to finish college and get his degree.

When Kori arrived in Seattle, she was miserable. Her apartment was so dismal, her classes were uninteresting, the weather was so cold and rainy. She had lost contact with her other friends so she could direct all her energy toward Paul. She felt so alone during the month of January. Paul's phone calls had been brief and infrequent, with tension traveling across the lines. She was so afraid he was going to tell her he didn't want her any more.

Kori became depressed and moody by the middle of the month. She didn't feel like going to class, and by the end of the month, her depression drained her. She didn't want to get out of bed and she nearly stopped eating. She completely lost her appetite and even the thought of food made her sick. She didn't want to talk to Paul or to her parents or to anyone at all. Nobody cared about her. She wanted to drop out of school. She stopped going to her classes.

Then she got really sick. She began to vomit every time she ate anything. She lost more than 25 pounds, and she didn't have much weight to spare in those days. She had no energy and she slept all day, every day. Thinking about food or smelling food made her sick, so for nearly two weeks, all she did was sleep.

Finally, she decided to go to the doctor. She felt like she was dying, so she needed to get her diagnosis and her prognosis. Did she have food poisoning or cancer or some other terminal condition? She didn't mind if she were about to die; her life was over anyway.

She was so cold, so sick, so weak from lack of nourishment, she didn't think she could drive – but since she had alienated everyone else in her life, she had to force herself to get dressed and drive to the doctor's office. This February morning just happened to be the coldest day of the year, with a brisk wind blowing and a beautiful, clear, blue sky. Although she was bundled in her warmest clothes with her hat and gloves, her teeth were chattering and she couldn't stand the feel of the cold seat against her back and legs. Her hands were so cold and the steering wheel felt like it was frozen, even through her gloves, but she had to touch it, to hold it, to turn it. She could see her breath in the car. Her nose felt like an ice cube in the middle of her face; her face hurt from the cold.

When she finally arrived at the doctor's office, she felt so faint and so ill, she had to go straight to the bathroom and vomit again and again, until nothing was left inside of her. She didn't know what happened next. She must have come out of the bathroom and gone into an exam room; or had she fainted and was transported to the exam room?

The next thing she could remember was lying on the table, shivering because she was so cold, waiting for something to happen. The whole scene was surreal: the brightness of the white cabinets causing her eyes to flicker; the thousands of dots on the ceiling, in patterns that begged for her to organize them in her mind and count them; the sickening poster on the wall, showing what happens inside the human body when a person smokes; the cold, hard, steel table beneath her; the nauseating odors in the atmosphere; the buzzing sounds of voices from the next room. Kori gripped the sheet that was covering her while she waited and waited, wearing just a paper gown.

Had they forgotten about her? Who had been examining her, a man or a woman doctor? Had she spoken to anybody? Was she dreaming?

She had no strength to move. She needed to get warm. Her body and mind wanted to go to sleep, but she was too cold. As she felt the cold air penetrating her skin, she imagined huge blocks of ice surrounding her.

Her stomach began to spasm of its own accord and she turned onto her side just in time to see a big metal bowl and she began to vomit again and again, into the bowl. Even though there was

147

nothing in her stomach, something was coming out of it, as if a battle were being raged within her, a sword fight or boxing match. Tears were flowing from her eyes when a woman in a white coat – Kori had never seen her before this moment – entered the room with a chart in her hand and a big smile on her face.

"Congratulations, Kori!" she said cheerfully, oblivious to Kori's condition. "You are pregnant!"

Kori understood the words she was saying, but she didn't understand it at all. She and Paul had spent only a few nights together, and they had been very careful.

She didn't hear anything else the doctor said. All she could hear was Paul's voice: "If you stay here and get pregnant, you will ruin everything for us. That would destroy our entire lives. You will ruin everything for us. That would destroy our entire lives. You will ruin everything for us. That would destroy our entire lives."

CHAPTER 33

She got dressed and drove home from the doctor's office, now so numb that she couldn't feel the extreme cold. She had ruined everything for them. She would not destroy their entire lives. Their lives did not have to follow the course they had set. They just needed to follow separate courses, starting today.

She was so sick. What about her parents? How could she tell them? They would also think she had ruined her own life if they found out she was pregnant. She couldn't tell them about it. She couldn't tell anybody about it. She was so sick and nobody knew and nobody cared. She didn't have a choice. Her new course was already set before her. She knew what she had to do. She had to do it immediately, before she got sick again, before she lost any more weight and faded to nothing.

She was still dressed, still wearing her coat and hat because even in her apartment, she couldn't get warm. She walked a few blocks to the clinic near the college and entered the building. A receptionist handed her some papers and explained something; Kori only heard the part about signing the waiver on the last page. The rest didn't matter. The only thing that mattered was eliminating her mistake, as soon as possible. She signed her name on the line and handed the papers to the receptionist. She sat in the waiting room with about ten other people. She didn't make eye contact with any of them.

"Kori?" a nurse said, motioning for her to follow her through a door.

Kori stood on her weak legs and made them walk behind the nurse, who took her into a room.

"Have a seat."

Kori sat.

"Are you sure this is what you want to do?"

Kori nodded.

"What about the father?"

"He is out of the picture."

"Are you married?"

"No."

"Did you discuss it with him?"

"I don't know who he is." The lie came out of her mouth so easily, as if someone else were speaking. She knew her face was expressionless.

The nurse made some notes on a paper.

"Are you sure this is what you want to do?"

"Yes, I am sure." She was more sure than she had ever been in her life.

"Do you have any questions about the procedure?"

"No." She couldn't think of any questions.

"This will be $125. You can pay cash, write a check, or use a credit card."

"Check," Kori said, taking out her checkbook. She wrote a check to the name taped to the counter and handed it to the nurse.

"Do you have someone to drive you home?"

"I live just around the corner." That was almost true.

"Come with me," the nurse said. She was neither kind nor compassionate, two traits Kori thought were required of nurses. She mumbled something about this not being an appropriate form of birth control, then she sighed, as if this were just part of the job.

Kori was taken to a large room divided into sections, at least six or eight sections, by curtains. Inside the third curtained stall, she was instructed to remove her clothes, slip into a hospital gown and get up on the table. She was freezing and her teeth were chattering. She tried to pull the gown around herself more tightly to get warm, but it wasn't working. The thought that this all would soon be over was the only thing that kept her going. She waited on the ice-cold table, aware of voices mumbling or softly crying in the other stalls.

"Okay, that's it," a lady's voice said. "You can get dressed and then go sit in there until you feel like you are ready to go. Take your time"

Kori heard sounds of paper crumpling as somebody moved on the table in the next tent-cubicle.

"Lie down," she heard the lady's voice say, a little closer to her than she had been a minute ago. "Scoot down and put your feet in here. Scoot a little more."

She heard more rustling and mumbling between a man and a lady, probably the doctor and nurse, then someone made a little yelp.

"You're okay, it's not that bad," the lady said. Kori heard sobbing, then she heard more rustling of papers and more mumbling.

"Okay, that's it," the lady said. "You can get dressed and then go sit in there until you feel like you are ready to go. Take your time."

Kori thought her turn would be next, but she again heard the nurse say, "Lie down," in the stall next to Kori's. "Scoot down and put your feet in here. That's good. You act like you have some experience with this."

She didn't hear anything from the next stall for a couple of minutes, but she could sense movement from there, and she heard more people entering the room and being taken into stalls. Kori was so cold, she pulled her knees close to her chest and wrapped her arms tightly around her body. She closed her eyes and almost went to sleep while she was sitting on the table.

"Wake up, this isn't a motel," a nurse told her, speaking very harshly. "Lie down," she said. "Scoot down and put your feet in here. Scoot a little more. Scoot down, I said, and put your feet in here."

Kori felt as if she were going to slide off the end of the table, she was so close to the edge. Her feet were contorted into some stirrups in such an odd position, her calves began to cramp and steel bars were pressing into her feet with extreme force. She didn't want to cry. This procedure was going to help her feel better and let her get her life back in its proper order.

A male doctor entered her stall and stood by her feet. The nurse handed him some instruments. Kori couldn't see what they were doing, and they were in such a position that her neck hurt when she tried to look at them, so she looked at the ceiling. She thought they should have put some kind of poster on the ceiling, a puppy, or some flowers, something, anything, to take her mind off of what was happening. She stared at the fluorescent light in the ceiling, watching it grow and shrink, glow purple and glow green.

The doctor's hands were large and skilled, but they felt rough and invading between her legs. She had had examinations before, but she had always gone to a woman doctor, one with small hands and a tender touch. Here, she could be a car engine, with his hands performing an oil change, bumping here and scraping there. Kori clenched her teeth. His fingers were just too large to be holding that instrument and twisting and turning and pulling and yanking in such a small area. She tried to breathe, then she felt an extreme cramp in her abdomen, worse than any cramp she had ever felt in her life. She blinked so she wouldn't cry.

"That's it," he said, and he left the stall.

"You can get dressed," the nurse said to her, handing her a large pad for the blood, "and then go sit in there until you feel like you are ready to go. Take your time." She left Kori.

"Lie down," the nurse said to the girl in the next stall. "Scoot down and put your feet in here. Right there, that's right."

Kori slowly moved herself up onto the table, her legs aching from being in such an awkward position, her feet hurting from pressing against the steel stirrups. She was completely drained now. She slowly put on her clothes, leaning on the table, resting every few seconds, unable to stand straight because of the cramps.

She made her way to a small recovery area that was crowded with about 20 chairs, and she sat in the nearest one. Several girls sat huddled in corners, holding hands with, presumably, their boyfriends. Kori was the only person who was there without anyone else. She tried to not look at the other people; they weren't looking at her. She didn't know anybody here. None of her family or friends knew she had come here. She unconsciously massaged the area where she was cramping when she realized, for the first time in nearly a month, she was not nauseated. She hadn't been able to eat anything for so long. Now she was extremely hungry.

She sat for a short or long time, she wasn't sure how long, while couples came and left the room, then she decided she was well enough to walk home. She didn't want to sit there all day. She was suddenly so very hungry! She wanted to get something to eat. As she left the clinic, she noticed a Kentucky Fried Chicken restaurant across the street, so she picked up a two-piece meal to take home and eat. She had never been in a restaurant that smelled so good! Just a few hours ago, any odor or scent made her feel sick. Her stomach was now growling instead of churning.

She wasn't sure how she made it home, but she did. She went into the kitchen, turned on the oven and opened the door – that was the only way she could quickly warm herself. She sat on a chair near the open oven and ate her chicken, biscuit, and mashed potatoes and gravy. When she finished eating this most rewarding meal, the first meal she was able to eat in weeks, she went to her room, wrapped herself in three blankets and promptly fell asleep.

CHAPTER 34

When she awakened, she didn't know what day or what time it was, but she did know she felt better than she had in a long time. She had been so sick for so long, and now she was recovering. She fixed herself a bowl of soup and a tuna fish sandwich, ate them in bed, and went back to sleep for another long session.

The next time she awakened, she was feeling quite good. She put the events of her sickness out of her mind. What had really happened, and what had been a dream?

She could never tell her parents what she had done. They didn't need to know. They considered her to be a good girl – she didn't need to ruin their image of her. The incident had ended with no problems, and they could keep being proud of her. If she were to confess everything, they would become angry with her; they would be ashamed of her. She would never be able to face them again. No, this mistake was hers, not theirs. She didn't want to hurt them.

Paul was going to be a problem for her. She couldn't tell him the truth, but she couldn't stay with him if she had this secret. He had practically told her they wouldn't be able to stay together if she were to get pregnant, that she would ruin their lives. Now she wasn't pregnant, but she could not live the rest of her life with him, knowing she could never tell him the truth, that she had been bad, that she had ruined their lives but she had taken care of the situation. She couldn't face him again, not ever. She could not lie to his face; she could not let him see this changed person, this liar. She wanted him to remember the good things about her, all the happy years, not the horrible mistake she had made, the mistake that had ruined their chance of a life together.

She would call him and end the relationship. No, she couldn't speak to him on the phone. She couldn't bear to hear his voice and know that she would never see him again. He knew her so well – he would know she was keeping a secret from him. She had experienced so much since the last time they spoke. He had sent her away from him. He didn't know how sick she had been. He didn't know what she had done to make sure their lives weren't ruined. He didn't know how strong she had become without him.

She quickly composed a letter to him, telling him their relationship was over. She read it several times, to remember what she was telling him, then she put it in the mail box before she could change her mind. She was doing the right thing. This was her best option. Her life was going in a new direction. She didn't need to be married to have a fulfilling life. All she needed was a good career, some friends, a nice apartment and a reliable car. A complicated relationship with a man was not necessary for her to find happiness in life.

She wrote a letter to her parents, telling them she and Paul were no longer a couple. She stated simply that she preferred to not share the details – and they never did ask her what had happened between them. She asked them to never tell him where to find her. They respected her privacy. They loved her and they accepted her as she was, a single person. She didn't have to be one half of a couple.

A few days after she mailed the letter, the phone rang. She knew it was Paul, and she refused to take his calls. She had stated in her letter that she wouldn't talk to him if he did call. She was afraid she would weaken if she heard his voice, and she could not allow that to happen: it was best for all concerned if she did not answer the phone.

Eventually, he stopped calling. When Kori had an opportunity that summer to do an internship in the production department at a TV station in Spokane, she gladly accepted the position. She concentrated all her efforts on learning everything she could about TV production. She put everything she had into doing the best job she could, and her supervisor was impressed with her work. At the end of the summer, before she registered for her classes for her senior year, she was offered a job at a sister station in North Dakota, a full time position in the production department. She gladly accepted it and she began her new life with her fresh start in September. She told her parents, as well as herself, that she would go back to college and get her degree, but once she arrived in North Dakota, she began to love her job at the TV station, and her freedom to live her own life and not have to consider anyone else when she had decisions to make. She was advancing in her career and living a very nice and pleasant life. She didn't need to finish college.

CHAPTER 35

Now Kori was looking back on her life and the choices she had made that year, seeing herself as the sinner God had seen. She had been so secretive about everything, she had thought nobody knew what she had done. As long as she didn't think about it, it was as if it had never happened.

However, God knew everything, each mistake, each lie. He knew every thought, the way she had changed things in her own mind to make herself seem righteous and Paul the bad guy, the way she had tried to hide from everyone else that she was a human who made mistakes and was not perfect – yet He still loved her and He comforted her now. He had been with her when she was so sick and nauseous. He had been with her in the doctor's office when she had learned she was pregnant. He had been with her at the clinic. He had been with her when she lied in the letter she had written to Paul. He had been with her when she erased her old life and made her fresh start. He knew the truth. Yet, He still loved her.

Kori knew she had to reconcile her old life with her new life in Christ. She couldn't live a lie with Christ right there with her, in her. She couldn't advance in her life until she finished her business from the past.

She understood the meaning behind her nightmares now – the Spirit of God made it so clear to her. She kept dreaming she had murdered someone but that no one knew because it was the truth, her truth. She had never allowed herself to think she had killed her own baby. She had always justified it by thinking of the abortion as merely 'a procedure.' She had not given herself time to think that she was carrying a baby inside her; rather, she had a problem and this was the only logical solution. She had never before considered that she had murdered Paul's baby.

She had not given Paul an opportunity to respond to the situation at all. She had been selfish to handle the problem without him. SHE had been the one to end the relationship; blaming Paul didn't make him be at fault. Putting the blame on him had merely eased her conscience from that time until now... but now she was allowing herself to accept the truth. She was guilty.

Kori had been so generous to announce in her heart that she had forgiven Paul, but in reality, she was the one who needed to apologize to him, and ask him to forgive her.

She had to tell him the truth; not just to get it off her chest, but to tell him what really happened. He deserved to know the truth. As she carefully considered what exactly she would say, she began to cry – not for herself, but for him. He had never known they had a created a child together; he hadn't known that she had their child exterminated, and in the process, she had also killed their future.

She had his phone number. Although she had made her parents promise not to tell Paul where to find her or anything about her, she had kept the Christmas cards he had sent to her parents. She had never thought she would ever want to contact him, but she wanted to have the ability, in case the opportunity presented itself. Today, right now, was her opportunity: more than an opportunity, her responsibility.

She dug to the back of her bottom dresser drawer, behind her pairs of pants, to a box where she kept the few letters and cards she received, and she found the Christmas card Paul had sent last year. She didn't know if he had ever married or if he had any other children. She had not let herself get curious about his life after they had gone their separate ways – or after she had gone her separate way, away from him.

She had to call him and explain everything to him, truthfully, and ask him to forgive her, now, while the Spirit of God was giving her strength and courage to do so.

CHAPTER 36

Kori opened the card and considered the phone number. What region of the country had that area code, she wondered. Yet, where he lived was not important: the truth was very important.

She dialed the number and heard his voice, unchanged, after all this time. She prayed for strength.

"Hi, Paul... this is Kori. How are you doing? Well, I have something I need to tell you..."

Novels by Dana Pride

Kissing a Dead Man
All These Things
Existing
No One Like You
Nightmares of Murder

Coming soon: The Red Cloak

For a list of all available titles, check Dana's website:
http://danabooks.8k.com

Everlasting Publishing
PO Box 965
Vancouver, WA 98666-0965
USA
http://everlastingpublishing.org

Other titles available:
Nathan is Nathan, by Jahla
Joseph's Journey, Volume 1, by Joseph Fram
Joseph's Journey, Volume 2, by Joseph Fram
Joseph's Journey, Volume 3, by Joseph Fram